IT ALL

BEGAN

with a mai tai

USA TODAY BESTSELLING AUTHOR

H.M. SHANDER

It All Began with a Mai-Tai

Published by H.M. Shander

Copyright 2020 H.M. Shander

Cover Design: GET COVERS

Editing: PWA & IDIM Editorial

Shander, H.M., 1975—It All Began with a Mai-Tai

Author's Note

At its heart, this is a beautiful romance

about finding yourself and true love.

However, within the pages are

descriptions of alcohol abuse, mentions of suicide,

toxic relationships, and a brief scene of sexual assault.

I've tried to be sensitive and delicate, but I understand these

words could reopen past scars.

Still, I trust you to know your limits and to read with care.

Table of Contents

Dedicated to my
fellow anthology mates from
Romantically Ever After –
we got our HEA!

Prologue

etween the slats of my resort-based plastic lounge chair I spied four empty plastic glasses. Each had been a delightful taste to the buds, cooling my insides with each gulp, because let's be real, no one sips the free booze offered at the resort.

"Hey, beautiful." His voice was deep.

Rolling over and pulling in my slim and nicely bronzed stomach just a little more, I seductively tipped up the brim of my hat and took in the familiar Adonis who'd pulled up a chair. His name escaped my lips, but Seth seemed to ring a bell. It was hard to keep them all straight. This week I'd thrown caution to the wind and hooked up with any piece of eye candy who showed the slightest interest. It was my vacation too, after all.

"Hey," I drawled out.

"Care for a drink?" In his sun-kissed hand was an

icy blue concoction. I'd had one of those earlier and it was delicious. "Sure, thanks." The ice-cold glass was heaven in my heated palms.

He tipped his glass toward mine before he downed it. Three gulps and it was empty.

Not to be outdone, I did the same. Damn, it went down smoothly.

"The guys and I are going to cross the bay and hang out at the Playa. Wanna come with?"

Hmm, it was a tempting request.

The Playa was the local hangout and not at all part of the resort. It was down the beach, over to the sister resort's dock where a motorboat took all of five minutes across the bay. The sandy beaches were plentiful, the drinks were much stronger than the resort-based ones, and also cost more than free, and there were also tonnes of people, likely lots of little children. I had parked myself in the quiet adults-only pool, tucked away from those yells and screams because I dealt with that all day long at work.

"You know what, I'm just going to hang here and work on my tan." I angled myself into a sensual pose, giving myself more of an hour-glass figure than I had. For good measure, I even stretched out my foot, pointing the perfectly manicured toes to help elongate my legs.

Stretching himself out across the distance between

us, he ran his giant hand over my hip and down my leg. "Later than?"

Clearly, his beauty eclipsed his brains and I itched to correct his speech but held myself back. "Perhaps." There was the after-hours bar. "See you at the disco for ten?" Seth was an incredible dancer with sensual dirty-dancing type moves. Just thinking about it was getting me all hot and bothered. Tonight's night cap would satisfy that urge.

"Yeah. Fer sure."

I watched his fine form disappear from sight. Yep, Seth had been a good distraction from the loneliness. A week on the beaches of Mexico and I'd had more attention than I'd received back home from my boyfriend of eight months. Yes, I was cheating on him, but he started it months ago. Since Christmas, he'd had an easy dozen different women. Our relationship clearly wasn't exclusive, but in my heart, I craved what my travelling companion and best friend was going through.

Our first day in Mexico and Tess met the most incredible guy. A true gentleman. So much better for her than the loser she finally dumped back home. Too bad this guy was only going to be a fling; he lived 3000 miles away from us. And what were they up to today? I wracked my slightly buzzed brain for what was on their activity list.

Turtle watching, was it? No thanks.

I reached up, stretching to readjust the giant umbrella to shade me, my bikini top inching higher and likely revealing a little under boob. From the corner of my eye, I saw an older guy drink me in and it made my heart flutter for a brief second. I knew nothing more than harmless staring would come from it; he wasn't my type and I had zero issues saying no. Still, I enjoyed the attention.

Under the expanse of the umbrella, the heat became tolerable again and I reached for my bottle of sunscreen. Slathering it over my heated body, I focused on the places the sun rarely sees, especially back home. My chest and stomach and hips and thighs were nicely protected, and since the guy was still watching, I took my time rubbing in the lotion.

I worked hard on my body and it showed. I wasn't body-builder buff, but lean and tight, with more of a dancer's body. My blonde wisps of hair escaped the floppy hat I wore perfectly, and the giant sunglasses gave me a mysterious celebrity-type essence. It was all part of a carefully crafted image, and those who truly knew me, knew it was all an act. At least I hope they did.

The air around me was pressing down, and another drink or two or three called out to me. Pulling the edge of my hat down and reducing my visibility, I flagged down the pool side server. I pulled out 50 pesos and held it up for him. "Can I get two of the blue and one of the pink drinks, please?" He'd been serving me drinks all morning and had an incredible memory. I, on the other hand, couldn't even remember the names of the drinks, just their colours.

"Si, gracias. Dios ocean tide and uno cabana." He walked away so silently I wasn't sure he'd actually left, but he had.

I stood slowly and readjusted my towel across the plastic webbing on my lounger, and pulled at my bandeau top, making sure everything was where it needed to be. Settling back onto my chair with my phone in my grasp, I crossed my legs at the ankle and beneath the cover of my sunglasses did a little people watching.

My server, who was exceptionally quick at bringing my drinks, returned and I handed him another 50-peso tip for his speed. He set them on the little table beside me and whispered out another Spanish thank you.

One by one, I drowned my desire to hang out with my bestie, while all the while wishing her total happiness with Jon. It was a weird feeling – I wanted her to enjoy the euphoria she was finally experiencing but at the same time, I was looking forward to quality girl time, something we hadn't had in a while. Being a grown up wasn't as rosy as I was led to believe. At least we checked in daily and I got the mini scoop on the fun she was having. I can't complain though, I too was enjoying the endless sun, the resort full of sun-tastic guys and the non-stop alcoholic drinks.

Four drinks in a short span were starting to take their effect, even as watered down as they were. Finally. Fuzziness was washing over me.

From the corner of my eye, I spotted a white-teed server, not my regular one though. "Excuse me." I waved him closer. "Could I get two Mai-Tais?"

He didn't move.

"Oh, I'm sorry." I dug through my bag, looking for the rest of my bills. I'd brought down five 50-peso bills and a couple of twenties. It wasn't even noon and I'd already used up all the higher bills. Begrudgingly, I pulled out a twenty. Such a cheap tip and hanging my head, I offered it up to him. "Sorry, it's all I have."

The bill left my fingers and I listened as he stepped away, worried he'd probably spit in my free drinks.

Resigned to that possibility, I allowed that wonderful relaxation feeling to settle over my body, the kind that happens when you've consumed a couple of alcoholic beverages in rapid order. It was going to be a lovely afternoon, free of thoughts and worries.

"Your drink, mademoiselle."

I knew enough foreign languages to know that was French, and the resort workers didn't *parlez francais*. I lifted the brim of my hat as the guy in the white shirt sat beside me.

"Bonjour." He smiled a wide, lazy smile.

Upon closer inspection, he was clearly not Mexican nor Spanish. He was as Canadian as me, although his colour had received a decent upgrade. A mop of dark wavy hair was pushed back off his forehead and he sported what had to be the makings of a vacation beard; more than a 5 o'clock shadow, less than a full out beard - that perfect amount of sexiness. But it was the eyes that did me in, once he removed his sunglasses. They were dark and sultry, and pulled me in like a tractor beam with their playfulness.

He handed me a cool drink which I took with a bit of hesitation.

"Thank you." More mature words escaped me. I blinked twice just to make sure he wasn't a server, trying to make me feel self-conscious. No, the idiocy was all on me. If I'd looked at him better, I would've seen that he was a tourist like me. There was no way he could've been mistaken for anything but. If it wasn't the farmer's tan peeking its way from under his shorts, it would've been the socks and sandals combo giving him away. Or the fanny pack. "About the drink order." My eyes fell to the condensation-laden mai-tai in his hand.

"Don't worry about it." He took a sip.

There goes my other drink. My gaze jumped from his dark browns back to the orange-coloured drink with a stab of cherry on top and back up again.

"Oh. Oh!" he said as his own gaze jumped between me and the drink in my hand. "Oh geez, this was meant for someone else." The lounger moved to the side as he stood quickly. "My apologies, I thought it was a pickup line. I'll go get you another one to replace this."

"No, it's fine." I sat up straighter and readjusted my sunglasses, blinking away the fuzziness that edged my vision. A dizzy spell washed over me and I reached my hand out in instinct to balance myself against his leg. Perhaps I was a touch intoxicated. Just a touch.

"You okay?" He removed my hand from the warmth of his cotton shorts and held it as he sat back across from me.

"Fine." I took a deep breath and tried focusing on the shrubs surrounding the pool area. On the umbrellas billowing slightly in the warm humid air. "I think I sat up too fast."

"This heat can be a real witch to the system, if you're not used to it."

"I've been here five days now. I'm totally used to the heat, and rather enjoy it."

I didn't miss the look as he gazed at the empty drinks beneath my lounger. "So, it's the booze then."

If I thought I could shake my head and not have it affect me, I would've done so and been convincing of it. But I knew better.

"I've heard the drinks on the adult-only side are more liquored than the drinks on the other side of that hedge. Just in case the kids steal a sip or two from their parents." He gave me a knowing nod. And truth be told, it made sense.

"I'll be fine in a few minutes." Or thirty. Maybe even an hour.

"So is your friend coming back right away?"

My friend? I was sure a dumb expression crossed my face. He lifted the glass. Right, he thought that was for someone else. "Oh, right. No. Not for a bit."

He glanced around the pool area, and whatever or whoever he was looking for, he gave a nod to. "Can you give me two minutes? I'll be right back."

"Sure, take all the time you need." I sure as hell wasn't going anywhere for the next little bit. I wasn't even going to attempt to lay down, lest my world start spinning.

I don't know where he headed, but he came back

right quickly and passed me a sealed water bottle.

"Drink this. Maybe we should get you into the water too, to cool down a bit. There's a shaded part over there." He pointed to the far end of the kidney-shaped pool.

I waved away his suggestions. "Honestly, I'm fine."

"Humour me. At least until your friend comes back. I don't think you should be alone."

"I'm okay."

"You could have heat exhaustion or sun stroke."

"I could also be nine sheets to the wind."

He laughed, the sweetest laugh I'd ever heard. "Well that proves it, because the expression is typically *three sheets to the wind.*" He rose and extended a hand to me. "Regardless, the cool water of the pool will help you feel better and when you've regained your footing, so to speak, I can make a better impression of myself."

I couldn't even begin to imagine that since he was already doing a pretty damn good job of charming me. "I'm Camille, by the way."

"Pleased to meet you. I'm Will."

Chapter One

The freeze-your-lungs-solid temperature in the covered jetway was a stark contrast to the sweaty, re-circulated tropical interior of the plane, unloading its Mexican tourists none too eager to step foot onto their native winter land. A forty-five-degree Celsius swing in the span of a few hours was not the ideal way to return home. Just lovely. Thankfully, I had the hindsight to pack a sweater in my carry-on bag, and I pulled it tighter across my chest.

I took a long look at my handsome and charming, albeit tired, travelling companion as we stepped off the jetway and wandered through the airport, over to the luggage pick up. Back on the resort, he'd been the guy who captured my attention the longest, and lucky for me, he lived across town.

"Anyone picking you up?" I asked Will. He

seemed like the guy who family was important to, and surely one of them would be there.

"My sister, Janet." He hoisted his carry-on bag over his shoulder and held my hand a little tighter. "You?"

I bit my lip. Normally, it would be my bestie, but she was still in Mexico. My family and I don't get along very well, and a few years back I raised some hell and was since abandoned. Oh well. It didn't bother me.

"I'm going to cab it home." And I hoped no one showed, although another friend had offered. I wanted the romantic fantasy; the one I'd watched on the tv screen. The long lingering kiss goodbye, foot tipped up in the air, the don't want to let you go waves, the promise of getting together again...

"We could give you a ride."

"That's really kind of you, but I'm on the west side and you're out in the Park district."

He gazed down upon me. "It's no big deal."

He was so sweet, willing to drive twenty-five minutes to my house and then an additional thirty to his. But it was too much. "I'll think about it."

"Excellent." He lit up like a Christmas tree. "You'll love my sister. She's super cool, and looks just like me, except she's feminine." I couldn't imagine the tall, dark-haired Will with any feminine features. Did his sister have a strong jawline with the more-than-a-hint of five o'clock shadow? I truly hoped not.

We got into the customs line and having cleared it, went over and grabbed our luggage. Will travelled light; one small suitcase. He pulled my industrial-sized pink bag—that I had to pay additional for—off the conveyor belt and smiled as he rolled it to me. That smile bagged me the first time I saw it spread across his face. Every time it happened, I was like putty in his hand.

"Just the one, right?"

I originally packed two suitcases, but my bestie talked me down to one big one. My pleas for another rolled off deaf ears. The horror of horrors if I was caught in the same dress twice in one week, vacation or not. Same with swimwear, although if I was honest, the bikinis didn't take much room. But she was right. Damn her. Nodding, I tugged on the handle of my suitcase and walked toward the main entrance where family and friends greeted you as if you were a famous celebrity. I thrust my weary shoulders back and tipped my chin up.

"We're still on for dinner Monday night?" he asked, stopping to let me pass first through the double doors.

"Absolutely." Our plans had been of a romantic nature; dinner at a quiet restaurant after a full day returning to work with an expensive bottle of wine, maybe a little nightcap afterwards…

"Great. I'll need to see a friendly face after work. It's tough meeting new colleagues."

"Where do you work?" That should've been a conversation we'd already had, but back in Mexico, it was nice to just simply enjoy the presence of another human being without having to fill the conversation with mindless chatter. Instead, we shared space, shared kisses and shared knowledge that we were comfortable with each other. For me, that never happens. But with Will, something just clicked, and we'd never advanced beyond second base.

The double doors automatically opened before he answered and the area before us was filled with loved ones, ready to welcome home their travelling friends and family. I was envious of them since no one stood there waiting for me. However, I still sauntered past the crowds, trying to appear as if I didn't care. I brushed the wavy strands of hair off my shoulders and put on a grin that I knew was a smidgen of alluring mixed with a bit of spice.

"There's Janet," Will said, giving my hand a little tug and pulling me away from the crowd that in my dreams thought I was someone famous.

I scanned the crowds looking for a mini-Will, and that's when I spotted it on the other side of the railing. A

14

large sign held above the crowd that read CAMILLE EVANS. Trey, my cheating boyfriend who'd been negligent on the romance as of late, stood smiling underneath it. Until he spotted me holding Will's hand.

"Oh damn."

Will pointed to the sign, his cheery disposition hitting the floor like a raindrop. "That's you?"

I nodded.

"And that's your brother, right?"

From the pitch in his tone, it was a question he hoped the answer was yes. I hated that I was going to disappoint him.

Three days. That's all I seemed I was going to get with perfect Will. With a guy who was tender and fun and didn't look at me like I was a piece of meat. Inhaling, and debating on lying, which was far beneath me, I answered with honesty. There was no hint of happiness in my voice, only disgust. "I can explain. That's my boyfriend."

Will released my hand faster than if he'd been shocked. "Seriously?"

I shrugged and a painful smile hung out on my lips. It was all I had left.

"Don't ever call me." He stormed a few feet away. "Ever." Turning around, he faced me, hurt crawling across his tight features. "I thought you were different."

I stuck my foot out and crossed my arms over my chest. No way was I going to look like the bad one here, even if I was. "You picked me up, remember?"

Will and I had met at the adults only pool when he walked by with a handful of drinks. I'd already had too much to drink and thought he was my waiter, so I flagged him down. He was wearing a white shirt like the other employees and had a thick mop of dark, wavy hair and a tan so golden, well, let's just say, he fit the part. It was an honest—drunken—mistake. Anyway, Will dropped off the drinks for his intended party friends and returned with the Mai-Tai I'd ordered. Upon closer inspection, he wasn't staff. They weren't built like lifeguards and firemen.

Will stared and his mouth opened, however, words failed to fall out. Instead, he took a step back and spun on his heel.

"Wait, I am different." But it was useless, and I was above begging.

He walked over to his shorter sister, who bore a slight resemblance to him, and the two of them glared at me. More so her than him.

A pitiful I-can-only-blame-myself sigh rolled out of me. What was done, was done. I knew better than to fight a losing battle.

Flipping my gaze in Trey's direction, he wasn't

looking thrilled either. The sign was on its side, and Trey was leaning on it.

"Hey," I groaned as I walked over. The suitcase came to a rest beside me and I sat upon it, the weariness of the day starting to take its toll. I should've been smarter to think that Trey would be affectionate after seeing me holding hands with another guy, but still. The fact that he didn't even lean in for a quick peck stung. I'd always kissed him after his indiscretions.

"Him? You were snogging him?"

Well… Will wasn't someone I snogged with. Not so much. He was more like an old soul trapped in a young man's body, a gentleman. Unlike the other resort guys I'd had the pleasure of meeting, Will was more of a hold your hand and kiss you at the end of the night kind of guy. Disappointingly, we hadn't even made it to third base, so the snogging part was still a possibility. Except now I'll never know how he was in bed, and he'll never learn how amazing I am. Yes, there were others at the resort, at the beginning. Two for sure, but to use Trey's favourite term, they meant nothing.

My head tipped to the side as I stretched out my aching neck muscles. "What's good for the goose is good for the gander." I met his glare head-on.

"For real?"

"Oh right, because you didn't the entire week I was away?" I laughed. "I may be blonde, but I'm not a complete idiot."

He pulled back in surprise.

My voice peaked. "Trust me, stud, I know more than you think I do. I know about Maria and Angelica and Jordyn."

It was fun watching him pale a little, especially since people mingled around us, checking out the conversation. He hated being the center of attention, where I loved it.

"Oh yeah, I know." Thanks to my little spy friend at the Pine Tree, I knew all about the indiscretions, and for whatever weird and wild reason, they never bothered me. I just kept a list of dates and times, and always wore a condom. I was the consistent one, the fall back one, the one he always returned to. And I was okay with that. However, I played his game while I was gone, and I had to admit, there was something fun about a different guy each day. No expectations for more. Just truly a wham-bam-thank-you-ma'am kind of fun. A revenge cheat. Or two.

Except, I hadn't planned on encountering a guy like Will. I didn't think I'd ever find a guy I could envision spending the rest of my life with. History said second best was all I was good enough for.

"What do we do now?" Trey just stood there, like a deer in the headlights. The sign was starting to curve under his lean.

Will and Janet had walked away without another backwards glance, and my heart ached with each passing breath. For a moment in time, even if it was only three days, Will had given me hope that I could be treated like a lady. That I was worthy of being treated so. He was the first guy in a long, long time who made the butterflies in my stomach soar and my heart beat a little faster.

In one fell swoop the fantasy was gone, and in its place was Trey. He was my fallback just as much as I was his, maybe even more so. A safety net that no matter what happened, he'd still be around. This incident was proof.

Exhausted from a day of travelling, a loud heaviness breathed out of me. "Take me home." I tugged on my luggage and headed toward the parking lot. "It's high time you and I discussed some things."

Chapter Two

$\mathcal{M}$y suitcase rolled against the closet door with a thud. I'd deal with it later. Like tomorrow or the next day. Right now, I needed a drink and a tall glass of maple whiskey on the rocks was calling my name.

Trey sat at the hand-me-down Formica table on the good chair; the one without all the peeling.

I grabbed the bottle of Crown Royal and filled two glasses with ice. "Help yourself." Trey poured in an ounce, whereas I made sure my ice cubes were well covered. I pounded back the first few sips and gave my lips a solid washing. "So… let's do this."

"Do what exactly?"

"I don't know. Aren't we supposed to solve our dilemma? You sleeping around, me having a little fun in Mexico."

He took a sip and shuddered. Whiskey wasn't his

jam, but he went with it. Most likely to appease me. There wasn't a strong bone in his body. Well, there was, but it was going to stay soft for a while. At least with me.

"How many were there?" Fine, he was starting first.

"That I snogged with?" I thought through the list of guys. It was enough to make my best friend Tess roll her eyes, and I saw her constant judgement in them. "There were only two. No, three." That I had a roll in the hay with. Four if you include Will and his 1910 ways, but there'd been no sexy times with him. Just the best kisses, the sweet way his hand wrapped around mine, the way he'd look at me like I was a beautiful flower and not a weed.

"Wow." Trey balanced his forehead in his palms.

"I don't need your number. I know." It was more than a handful. Someone did not miss me at all. The ice cubes bumped against my top lip while I tipped the rest of the amber-coloured fluid into my expectant mouth. Ah, ice cubes. That brought to mind the fun I'd endured with... God, what was his name again? Ah, it doesn't matter. But we had fun in my room with the bucket of ice.

Trey kept his focus on the alcohol. "So, are we breaking up?"

There were so many smart-assed answers I wanted to give him, instead, when I looked at him all I felt was sadness. Trey wasn't an awful person. A cheater, definitely, but he wasn't a bad guy. He was sweet and helpful and generous with his time. A good friend for sure. It was his romantic relationship skills that needed work. However, it wasn't all his fault. "Does that scare you?" *Like the way it scared me?*

"Maybe." He looked at me briefly before dropping his gaze to the table. "I like you."

"And I like you." I reached for the bottle of whiskey, refilled my glass and took another shot. "But I'm confused."

"About?"

"Us." It was the truth. "I wasn't bothered when you were with the other girls, and I didn't feel bad when I was with the guys but the whole time, or at least a good chunk of the time, I missed you while I was gone. Despite what I did, I did think about you." Until I met him. Will. My shoulders rolled inwards. "That's why I'm confused. I'm not bothered by what you did, nor about what I did, but at the same time, I know it's unhealthy to be in a relationship like this, and yet…" I sighed. "I don't want to let you go." I took another sip. "Did you ever feel guilty about cheating on me?"

He shrugged and wobbled his glass, making little circles on the table. "Just the first time."

22

"Was it exciting for you?" The alcohol was starting to kick in and I was feeling the little tingles in the pit of my stomach. Hadn't felt them all day – it was too damn expensive to drink on the plane and my morning intoxication had worn off rather quickly. "I mean, for me, it was kind of a thrill."

He made eye contact and gave me a solid staring.

"I know it makes me a cheater, even if you did do it first." And that'll be my brand – the cheater. That's what Will thought, I was sure of it. If I were to ever see him again, that'll be the first thing he'll remember about me. Not the fun in the pool. Not hanging out sipping pink drinks under the heat of the sun. Nope, my boyfriend showing up at the airport will be how he remembered.

"Do have any remorse?"

Trey's honest question brought me back to the present. He deserved an honest answer. It was the least I could do. I shook my head. "None." Except for Will. I wanted more with him and it sucked that I got caught before I could end things with Trey. "Did you ever?"

"A couple of times, but it passed quickly."

I finished my second glass and reached for the bottle.

Trey pulled it away.

I gave him a look and leaned over the table,

yanking it from his weak grip. "What happened to us? We used to be all over each other, and now, we're barely hanging on."

"I don't want to break up." There was an innocence about him that made me feel guilty for even thinking it. As if this was the first time he was about to be dumped.

"I don't either but at the same time, I don't want to call you my boyfriend. That title used to mean something."

He blinked a few times. "Really? You don't?"

Well, shit. Why was I feeling so bad about this? He cheated first, not me. I should've kicked his ass to the curb months ago, after the first known hookup. "No. We're not that way with each other anymore. We haven't gone on a romantic date in so long." Listening to Tess share with me the blooming romance she had going on, fired the jealousy bug in me. When was the last time Trey treated me like a woman, and not a fuck friend? Months.

"So, we are breaking up." It was a statement, not a question, as if he knew it was coming and by pleading with me, I'd stop the inevitable. You can't stop a sinking ship by bailing it out; it only prolongs the despair.

"I guess so, although maybe that ship sailed a long time ago." The ice in my glass twirled around with each motion and I took a sip when there was enough fluid accumulated in the bottom. "Unless you can name a reason for us to stay together?"

"I like you."

I shrugged. "There should be more than that, don't you think?"

Trey sat there, shifting in his seat and the only sound escaping him was a quiet moan. Almost like it was hurting him to remain silent and share space with me while our future hung in the air. I'd dangled the carrot of opportunity in front of him and he didn't even see it.

He folded his hands together. "What about sex? Can we still enjoy that with each other? Have a meet up once a week or something?"

Sex had always been something we really rocked at, but I shook my head and avoided eye contact. Having been with others, ones who shattered me repeatedly and for hours at a time, Trey was a one-trick pony whose moves would likely no longer wow me. The parting had to be total and complete, it was for the best.

Trey stood and dumped his glass in the sink. "Well, I guess I'll see you when we pass each other in the hall or something."

The joys of living in the same building. "It's better this way." At least that's what I was going to tell myself. Daily. Hourly. Whatever it took, because I did love Trey, I just wasn't in love with him. Anymore.

Once Trey was outside in the hallway, I closed and locked the door. It felt good to cut him loose, sort of. Although now I was going to be all alone. I yanked open the door. "Trey?"

He stopped and spun around, a sparkle of hope dancing across his face at the mention of his name. "Cammy?"

"Why don't you stay the night and we can reassess in the morning?"

A charming smile spread from cheek to cheek as he practically ran to my apartment.

That would be better. Maybe in the morning with a clear head, I could cut him out of my life. But for now, I wanted the company, and being with Trey was better than being alone.

Chapter Three

Tess slumped down on her sofa and took one of her fancy throw pillows and covered herself with it. Her face was tight, and her shoulders rolled in. I hated seeing her in so much pain and heartache, but I did warn her that it was bound to happen, and she should give herself some distance from Jon. But did she listen to me? Not this time.

"So, T-bird, what fun activities did you do on the resort after I left?" Tess took a ten-day trip to Mexico, where I could only afford the weeklong.

"I read. Tanned by the infinity pool. I even went parasailing." Her eyes got a little brighter, even if it was brief.

"Shut up. You did not."

She reached for her phone off the coffee table and thumbed through. "Look here's a video of it."

Well, I'll be damned. If it weren't for her infectious

giggle on the video, I would've sworn it was someone else strapped to a parachute on the stern. Mesmerized, I watched as the boat slowly released her into the air. "I can't believe you did that."

"I couldn't either. But it was so much fun. Everything looks so different when you're that high up."

I shook my head. "Look at you. All wild and hunting for adventure."

She lowered her head and tossed the phone onto the table. "Sure."

I rubbed her back. "I know he was important to you. Are you and Jon still going to talk?"

"Yeah. But trying a long-distance relationship? That's going to be so hard. How are we going to manage? I want to see him and hold him and breathe him in." She closed her eyes and leaned her head against the top of the couch. "It was the million little things he did and said that made me swoon, more than his drive for adventure."

I sighed. For a few days, they had the most perfect romance. He brought her out of her shell, and I think she did the same for him, but I can't be sure. I didn't know him before the trip and to be honest, I didn't see them much over the trip either. However, I did see the magical effect the vacation romance had on my bestie.

I gave Tess's arm a rub. "Yeah, he was pretty

amazing. But so are you. Of all the women at the resort he could've hit on, he choose you. You! And I'm not surprised. Look at you. Jon was even impervious to my charms." I attempted the standard eyelash batting and gentle flirting that worked on just about every guy, except him. That boy had eyes only for my T-bird.

"Speaking of which." She straightened herself and faced me. "What's up with you and Trey? Did you dump him?"

"We're still figuring that out." He stayed over two nights out of three, and although we're not going on any dates, we're having a lot of sex. And who knew, he learned a couple of new things that tantalized me.

"But you came home with that guy."

"Will," I filled in the name for her as I hadn't properly introduced them. There hadn't been time. "He dumped me at the airport."

"Oh, Camille."

"It's okay. Trey was waiting to surprise me. Well, it worked." I hopped off the couch, not wanting to discuss Will anymore. It wasn't right to have an achiness in my heart after just a few days. Into her kitchen I went. "Do you have a beer or something?"

"There should be a hard lemonade in the back of the fridge."

I pushed aside all her smoothie concoctions and bags of fresh fruit and found the sought-after liquor. "Found it." I wiggled the bottle to show her. "Want to split it?"

"No thanks."

I twisted the lid off and dropped it into the garbage.

"So back to you and Trey." Her focus never left me.

I folded myself into one of her sofa chairs and pulled my legs up. "There's nothing to tell. We both know what happened when I was away and we're both cool with that." I took a long pull on the bottle. Geez, that cold liquid felt nice slipping down my throat.

"Camille, you deserve so much more than you're getting."

"I'm getting exactly what I deserve, trust me." There were things about me that not even my best friend of twenty plus years knew. And it wasn't that I didn't trust her with that secret, it's that I didn't trust myself with saying it. Knowing just painted you with a different brush, and I didn't want that from Tess. She accepted me for who I allowed her to see.

"Awe. You need to think better of yourself, really. If you could see yourself the way others do…" She squeezed the oversized throw pillow in her lap.

I turned away from the pitiful look on her face. "I know what they see because I work hard at making sure they do. Do you think they'd be attracted to my body if there was an ounce of flab? No way. So, I stick with my hundred sit-ups and crunches daily, and I do the lunges until my butt begs me to stop. I make sure to wax away any hairs and that my hair stays the right shade of blonde with the perfect amount of foils. Even my lipstick is the right shade of pink." And that's why there was hardly any money left over at the end of the month. Upkeep was draining on the bank account.

"There's more to you than your body. You have a big heart and you're so smart." Her voice weakened, but I knew why. We both knew better; it was lip service.

"Sure." Tess was the smart one, I was the pretty one. It was how we survived middle school and high school. She got all the scholarships while I was voted the most popular. She was a saver and spent her money wisely, living well within her means, where all my money went to the salon. Tess was everything I wanted to be. And will never be.

Tess threw the pillow to the side and dropped her feet onto the floor. "I want to talk about something serious with you for a minute, okay?"

I braced myself, keeping my tone light. "About?"

Her gaze fell on the half-drained bottle of hard lemonade. "Your drinking."

"Sorry. I took the last one. I'll get you more before the weekend."

Her hand waved through the air. "Nonsense. I'm not concerned with that. At all." She closed her eyes and took a breath. "I'm concerned with the drinking aspect."

I laughed. "You think I have a drinking problem?" It was absurd to hear it out loud. Laughter punctuated the air again. "I don't think so."

Her steely-eyed gaze roamed over me. "You drank excessively at the resort–"

"Because it was part of the experience." I rolled my eyes. "Everyone knows that. You go to Mexico and eat to your heart's content and drink until you pass out."

She shook her head and turned all motherly. "How much weight did you gain then?"

Busted. Tess knew I was a daily weigh-in type of girl. As much as I indulged in all the tasty offerings, my weight gain was zero. But, in my defence, I also have a wicked metabolism.

"See? I gained five pounds."

A deep roar of laughter rolled out of me. "Where?" It wasn't possible. Tess had been too busy with her new adventure to eat much. For as often as I joined her at meals,

32

there wasn't a lot of food consumption. "You look great, as always. Maybe that weight gain you're complaining about is all the heartache you're carrying around."

"Nice try, but it won't work."

"What won't?" Playing dumb was a trick I'd learned back in high school. It got me out of a lot of trouble.

"Mi, I care about you. I know you think no one does, but I love you like a sister."

Words to cut my heart with. Tess had been my only form of family.

"I'm watching you because I care. I don't want you to harm yourself."

I scoffed. "A drink every now and then isn't harming myself."

"You know what I mean."

Sadly, this was true. I sighed.

Tess readjusted herself on the couch. "Alright, talk over."

Thank god for that.

"You know what I think we should do? Let's join a club or something? Izabella wants something to do once a week too, and I figured it would be fun for the three of us girls to hang out weekly."

Izabella was our other mutual friend. We never saw

each other as often as we'd like since she lived near downtown and Tess and I lived on the city's edge. It didn't help that she spent all her time in the lab either. She claimed she was going to solve some of the world's most pressing medical concerns.

"Really?" I raised my perfectly manicured eyebrow at her.

She inched to the edge of her seat. "Yep. Iza is up for just about anything, but suggested a writing class, or a book club or a dance group."

"Okay, now I know you both have gone off the deep end. A dance class? That's so not you." I tipped back the hard lemonade.

A dreamy look settled over her face. "That's the best part. It'll get us out of our funk."

I wasn't in a funk. "Not going to happen." Because for one, money. Money that I didn't have to spend. And two, I couldn't picture Tess taking dance lessons. They don't teach dance club style of dances, they teach ballroom. Way too old fashioned, even for my best friend and besides, Tess was known for having two left feet.

"There'd be cute guys."

"At a book club? Yeah right. Maybe at ballroom lessons, but they'd be old balls. No thanks."

"What about an astronomy club? Lots of nerds I'll

34

bet." She nodded her head.

I finished off the hard lemonade. "Nerds aren't my type so it's not going to happen, T-bird. But," I reached out and patted her leg, "never stop trying."

"I just hate for you to feel so … miserable and with someone who doesn't compliment you."

"Are we back to talking about Trey?" Because I was so over that. And he did compliment me. In fact, several times last night he told me how much he loved my body.

"I don't know, are we?" Her eyebrow went sky-high, and she tipped her head knowingly to the side.

"We're not." I stood and added my empty bottle to her recycling pail. "Besides, I could get a hundred other guys."

"Like who? One of your co-workers?"

No way. The only guy close enough in age to me was as gay as the morning sun was bright. I flipped through the list of guys I saw daily. "What about a parent? That one dad at school is always shamelessly flirting with me. I could give it a go."

"Major conflict of interest."

That was true. It would look wrong on so many fronts, especially since his daughter was in my class.

"Come on. Let me find something fun for us to

take. No pressure to find a guy, just stretch ourselves out a little and see what happens. Embrace a new and improved life."

I crossed my arms over my chest and stuck my foot out. "And you're going to look for a guy?"

"Well... ah..."

"Exactly." Not that I blamed her. Jon was perfect for her, just too damn far away.

"But let's do something different. I don't want to be boring Tess anymore, I tossed her away in Mexico and found myself. I want to live life and explore and learn and see what the world can bring me."

As much as I was envious at the positive change in my bestie, I was proud of her and excited for her new horizons. "Wow. You really have changed."

"I know I have." She tapped her chest. "And it feels so good. You can change too. You deserve so much more than you get."

"As you've said." I grabbed the keys off the counter, it was time to go home. A pile of prep work for my class waited for me.

Tess came and stood in front of me. "Please. Just one class." She'd reduced herself to begging and giving me puppy-dog eyes. Damn her.

I studied her pleading face filled with hope and

longing. How could I say no? If I gave her free reign to plunge headfirst into this, no doubt she'd find something off the wall and fun. I mock pouted. "I'm just giving you a heads up. I won't enjoy this."

Tess smacked my arm playfully. "You don't even know what I have in mind."

"Yeah, well."

"So, you'll do it?" She was bouncing on the balls of her feet with excitement.

"Fine. But you have to keep the costs down. A kindergarten teacher's salary isn't big."

"Promise." She crossed her heart with a smile that I was happy to see on her beautiful face.

I planted a kiss on her cheek. "Let me know the details." I waved as I exited her apartment. Tess was amazing. A bit of a goody-two-shoes, but still she was no wizard. And it would take a spell of astronomical proportions to get me to change.

Chapter Four

The week had been arduously long, and it was only Friday morning. Just needed to get through today because tonight, Tess and I were going to a lounge. Not the usual club but some jazzy bar she'd read about in the YEG Arts Highlights. The girl was out to broaden her horizons, and I was tagging along for the ride.

Before the school day had even started, our principal had pulled me aside.

A robust man with a head full of grey hair, he reminded me a bit of Colonel Saunders, minus the goatee. Didn't help that his last name was Saunders either. He also wasn't very approachable, and anytime he stepped into my kindergarten room, I braced myself for bad news.

"Good morning, Miss Evans."

I dropped the piles of pre-cut strips of paper for today's art project and nodded a hello.

He waddled over to my desk and cleared his throat. "As you know, Jesse has fallen ill and is on emergency medical leave." Jesse was the other kindergarten teacher, and as such, we collaborated on a few projects. It sucked that something undisclosed had taken her away from us. She was a valuable member of the team. "A temporary sub was contracted, and as the higher man on the totem pole, if you will, I need you to lead by example and give our new recruit a helping hand."

I found it completely laughable, but of course stayed professional, as I was practically a newbie myself. I'd only been teaching full time this year; my first two years I'd been subbing around. "Sure. What do you need me to do?"

"Help out however it's needed. He's got experience with kids from his district, just not any this young. It will be new territory for him. He has no teaching plan set up yet either, so share with him what you and Jesse were working on."

I sighed but agreed. Guess that meant she was gone for the rest of the year and there were still twelve more teaching weeks left. "When will he be here?"

"He'll be here before the bell with any luck." Mr. Saunders cleared his throat.

"What's his name?"

"Liam. Liam Donaldson."

I shrugged and sighed. Liam was a common name with the little kids or considerably older men. The sub was probably old-balls and set in his way, and would make the remaining weeks miserable because he didn't think the littles needed any technology in their lives, even though that was where the future was headed. Probably one of those who thought they should be in desks and not running around. One sub, who *was* old-balls, actually scoffed at the idea of flexible seating. But that was the old way. Like everything else, education is always evolving. "Okay, thanks." I wasn't looking forward to this. The end of the year was going to suck. Why did Jesse have to get sick?

After the principal left, I finished my set up and went to see if this Liam had shown yet. I wandered to the room across from me and went to put my hand on the doorknob. It was already unlocked as the door was opened a crack. Good sign. I poked my head into the class to see who was inside critiquing his temporary class. That form. That hair. No fucking way! I immediately pulled back, banging my head into the door and letting out a "Son-of-a-bitch."

I rubbed the sore spot on the back of my head and hightailed it to my class.

"Excuse me, miss. Are you okay?" His voice was

like sugar, sweet but a little rough.

I stopped and debated turning around. The last time we saw each other, it ended terribly.

His footsteps approached. "Miss?"

Inhaling a large amount of courage, I spun on my two-inch heels and dropped my hands to my side. "Hi, Will." I emphasised the name he'd used at the Mexican resort.

His expression fell. Guess I wasn't who he was expecting either. "It's William, actually. But I go by Will to my friends and Liam to my colleagues." There was more of a disenchanted smile than anything else on his face. "So, you're the Miss Evans who's assisting me."

"In the flesh."

He studied me up and down, not in an uncomfortable way, more like cautiously, as if he were unsure how to proceed.

Taking the lead, I inched over to him, smoothing out the lines on my skirt and ensuring my scarf was in the right position. "I promise you, here, I am the epitome of professional." My tone was more clipped than I anticipated, but for some reason, I felt on the defensive. "You have nothing to worry about, but I'll tell you something…" I stepped closer to him. "What happens beyond those doors, stays out there. I don't bring it to work, and I'd appreciate it if you did the same." It's not like we were a serious item or anything at the resort, so it was a relief to me that I had nothing to be embarrassed about with regards to us having already met but still... If he saw me with other guys it might look bad to the higher-ups if they ever found out. I'm sure Mr. Saunders expected my sweet kindergarten persona to follow me around.

"Yeah. No problem." He inched backwards a little, his colour changing just enough to be noticeable.

"Great. Now that that's settled, my room is right there." I pointed to the door across from his. "Did you want your herd of kids to join mine until recess and I can help you get settled then?"

"You know what?" He took a deep breath and readjusted his tie. "That would be super. Gives me a chance to see what things are like."

"Fabulous." I flashed him my work smile, the kind that was meant to be warm and friendly. Tess told me it was the fakest smile going, but there weren't many reasons to smile one of the true smiles lately. "You head in there and I'll round up the herd as they come in."

The bell rang and forty-one eager, chatty students filed into my space, trampling over each other for a spot on the carpet while Mr. Donaldson sat on the chair in front of them, acting like he belonged in this space. It was going to be a long morning.

"Thanks for all your help, Miss Evans." At recess, Mr. Donaldson and I had set up his workstation and brought up his list of students. Thankfully, he was familiar with the system and took to it like a duck to water. I don't know why I'd worried so much. It had been great leaning over his shoulder and navigating him through the important icons on his desktop. I could breathe him in, without it seeming stalkerish. He still smelled good, a relaxing kind. No cologne as it was against school rules, but definitely a fresh shower smell.

I clicked out of the program, brushing my hand against his bare arm. Gently, I'd suggested he ditch the tie and suit jacket, saving those for special events, and literally roll up his sleeves. Kindergarten wasn't the place for nice suits, especially dry clean only ones. On more than a couple of occasions, I'd been someone's personal tissue and I was thankful for wash and wear clothing.

A staff list appeared on the screen. "Here's a list of staff and their classrooms. I'd familiarize yourself, especially the grade one teachers. You'll be doing a lot of collab with them in June to help get your herd ready for September." I stretched out and smoothed down my skirt, walking toward the door. I wanted a quick snack before the bell and forgot to bring it over with me.

"Miss Evans, can I ask you something?" He rose and strode across his room, sidestepping the alphabet carpet.

"Sure."

He stood impossibly close and my heart skipped a beat while I stared into the depths of his eyes. "Why do you address your students as a herd?" There was a hint of annoyance to his voice.

I shrugged, my annoyance replacing the lust. "I don't know."

"Well, it bothers me."

Oh geez, a sensitive staff member. "It's not meant as anything insulting, they just remind me of a herd of cats. Ever try to round up more than four? It's impossible." I would know. My cat, years ago, had a litter of seven and that was chaos. I saw the students behaving in the same manner.

But Mr. Donaldson did not seem pleased. His brow was furrowed, and his thick hair almost seemed to stand at attention when he raked his hand through it.

"Would you prefer I address them as a group of students? Or a cluster?"

"Either of those is preferred to herd, although class

is the generally accepted term."

"Fine, class." I ran my gaze over this man. How could he have been so sweet and charming in Mexico and such a stick in the mud here? What a difference. "Anything else that bothers you?"

He opened his mouth. There was more to come, and I braced myself for it, but he snapped his jaw together when the bell rang. "If I think of anything, I'll let you know."

"I'll try to keep myself from getting excited while I wait." I strolled to my class, making sure I had a little more spring in my step.

"Oh, there you are," a high-pitched voice bellowed out behind me.

I turned to see school flirt sashay over to her fresh blood. "Hi, I'm Shannon O'Daughtry, but you can call me Miss Shannon." She put way too much emphasis on *miss*. "I teach the third grade just down that hall, and if you need any help at all with anything," she tipped her mousy brown head full of curls back and stuck out her ample chest, "you just holler. I can help you find the best places to eat and shop."

"That's kind of you, Miss, but I'm from Sherwood Park. I know my way around the city."

"Even better." She borderline purred.

"Aren't your students coming in, Shannon?" I asked and put my arms across my chest, unsure of why it bothered me so much that she was being over-the-top with him. It's not like I had any claim to him, but sheesh, the guy just started here.

"They have music. I'm in no rush." She narrowed a wing-tipped eye in my direction.

"Yes, well, it was lovely to have met you, Shannon, but I need to get my students. Please excuse me." Mr. Donaldson side-stepped the teacher and opened his door further as the trickling of noise and little people made their way toward their classrooms.

Shannon huffed off and satisfied that she was out of sight for now, I took off into my own room to welcome back my herd, er, class.

Chapter Five

*A*s if Fridays didn't drag as it was, the day never ended. Mr. Donaldson hardly spoke more than a few words in my general direction, which was just fine by me. It was better that way especially since he had ended it and hadn't even bothered to hear my explanation. Trey and I were already on the fritz before I went to Mexico, so it's not like I was cheating on him anymore than Trey was already cheating on me. We just hadn't outright agreed to see other people. But that was all over now.

Trey and I had only hooked up a couple of nights this week. No dinners, no movie dates, nothing that would suggest we were a couple. And Liam or Will or William, whatever the hell name he wanted to be called, there had been serious boyfriend potential with him. But not now. Sad as it was, because I really had enjoyed his company in Mexico and on the plane ride home, it was over.

Time to move on.

And the Soul-to-Soul Lounge was my hangout for the night and the location for my prowling. Izabella mentioned it to Tess, in her sudden dire need to expand her horizons, thought it would be a neat thing to try. I wanted to get wrapped in her enthusiasm and see first-hand how this would play out. Probably a total bust, but then again, I was seeing a new side of her. She was happy, mostly, and was changing her life around. It's a crying shame that Jon was only along for the ride from a distance. Four thousand kilometers of distance.

And she'd be picking me up in twenty minutes.

I danced my way to the kitchen and poured myself a tall glass of whiskey-neat and downed it in record time. A pre-drink was the best choice to start the buzz going before paying the ridiculous price of a bar drink. Three ounces of those bad boys and I could've bought the whole 26-ounce bottle. It was highway robbery at its finest.

The glass tipped onto its side as it fell into the sink, but not giving a shit, I ran to my room and did a once over. A tight green dress highlighting my perky breasts in the best push-up bra I had. Check. No panty lines. Double check. Thank god for thongs. Black heels. Yep. My makeup was pristine, and my hair looked amazing thanks to that new tool that curls your hair perfectly the first time.

I gave myself finger guns. "Looking good." Confident I was ready to party with the ladies; I grabbed my handbag and met my friends in the lobby.

The lounge was a far cry from what I'd anticipated. The median age of people was pushing fifty, like twice my age, and the atmosphere was one of darkness and heavy velvet drapery. I expected a small club setting just with jazz music, not a corner stage that was the same size as the eating area in my apartment and a half dozen tables surrounding it. The place was tiny. And talk about overdressed. I looked like a streetwalker compared to the others who were sporting jeans and shirts. Even Tess, who was a knockout in her halter-top dress I'd seen her wear in Mexico, was on the overdressed side. Izabella seemed to have taken a page from the same book I did and dressed herself in a sparkly hi-lo dress. Yep, we were three women on the prowl. Well, two of us were.

Tess beamed. "This place looks amazing, eh?" She side-stepped over to an empty table and sat down. "This is impressive."

If you say so.

I grabbed the seat beside her and crossed my legs. My chances for sex with a random stranger went out the window. Scanning around the room, the guy closest in age to me was at least mid-thirties, but he had his arm wrapped tightly around a voluptuous blonde, so I instantly ruled him out. I had some standards. Not many, but enough.

Tess flagged down a server and ordered herself a drink. She turned to me, but I'd been too busy checking out the lack-lustre guys to hear what she ordered. However, Tess was usually pretty mild with her drink choices as she was a featherweight when it came to alcohol.

"I'll have whatever she ordered."

"Really?" Tess raised her eyebrow and turned her attention toward the stage.

"Bring me a cosmopolitan," Izabella asked. "Please."

That sounded good. Maybe for my next drink. I had brought enough cash to cover me for three mid-priced drinks and an appetizer.

A spotlight focused on the five people who had miraculously appeared with their instruments and took their spots on the raised platform. A piano played and the horns started tooting along in tune. Surprisingly, it wasn't too bad. The singer, a beautiful lady with a Jessica Rabbit look, belted out a song in the deepest voice I'd ever heard from a woman, and it was soulful.

Tess nudged me with her elbow. "What do you think?"

"You know, it's not awful."

She glared at me.

Izabella smiled. "I have to agree with Cam. It's not too bad." She gave me a wink.

Tess's gaze floated down to my half-full drink on the table.

Before she could comment on it, I spoke up. "You know, it's not the worst place to hang out on a Friday night, even if we are the youngest people in here." I glanced around again to prove my point.

"You need to step outside yourself."

"Have you been hanging out with crystals and voodoo, because you're talking really weird. A couple of weeks ago, this wouldn't have been a place you'd have ventured to either." I took a paced sip from my drink and avoided that sympathetic, downward turn of her smile.

"You're right, and I'm sorry."

I certainly didn't feel any better watching her expression fall. This was supposed to be fun for her, and here I was ruining it. "It's not that bad, I'm just being a bitch. It's what I do best." I touched her arm to get her attention.

She studied me and gave me a solid once over.

"You had a bad day today, didn't you?"

"It was just long and different. We got a new sub in and I'm stuck with the training and showing them around and basically making them feel welcome in the school."

Izabella smiled and brushed her long hair over her shoulder. "That shouldn't be too hard for you, you're a sweetheart."

I dismissed her comment. Normally, no, it wouldn't be. But because it was *him*, it was completely different. All day long, I was on the defensive, ready to lash out.

"What grade?" Izabella ran her fingertips up and down the stem of her cosmopolitan.

"Kindergarten."

"Oh gosh, that should be real easy."

"You'd think." I rolled my eyes. But it was true. Kinders listened, for the most part, and didn't look at you like a bug to be squashed. When I did my training, I was put into a middle school room for six weeks, and that was hell. Those kids were mean.

"Is she nice?" Tess asked.

I could've stated that the new sub was a male, but with Tess, that would lead to more and more questions. Likely ones I didn't have the answers to. So, for the first time in a very long time, I lied, and I don't know why. I wasn't ashamed, and it's not like he ever saw me naked, but it's weird. "I don't know her well enough to answer that."

Izabella frowned. "What kind of answer is that?"

"Well... maybe she's nice, but she just rubbed me the wrong way this morning. And then Shannon hit all over him. I mean her."

"Him? Your new sub is a him?" Tess's eyes sparkled more than was necessary and she swept her bangs off her face as she leaned in. "Is he cute?"

So hot. Model cover sexy. It was a shame I hadn't peeled him like a banana back in Mexico. It had been so easy with the others. "Meh." But he wasn't attainable anymore.

"Really? That's too bad."

Izabella added. "A man who works with young kids. Total swoon-fest." She fanned herself for added effect.

"It is what it is." As in never going to happen. I tried to ignore the look she was giving me. Tess knew better, and it was written all over her face. "Let's listen. I like this song."

The band played a cover of a Meghan Trainor song with a wildly funky jazz beat, and it was quite something.

I found myself watching the lead singer twist and turn on stage as she smoothed her hands down her sparkly dress and out to the side.

"That one was pretty good." It wasn't a beat I thought anyone could dance to, at least not from the clubs I'd frequent, but the crowd around us sure loved it. They cheered and sang along. Tess included.

By the time the band finished their first set, I'd had the luxury of sipping two more drinks and was feeling nicely buzzed. However, I'm pretty sure the alcohol affected my hearing, because as they were introducing the band members, the lead singer, who was named Gigi, said the piano player was the king of the ivory keys. And called him by name.

Liam Donaldson.

Chapter Six

*M*y mouth hit the floor, and I shook my head in wonder. Of all the gin joints in all the world, I had to be in *this* one and he had to play here of all places.

The musicians stepped off the stage as the house lights came on and following Gigi, stopped at various tables to shake hands.

I stood rapidly. "I think we should go, Tess."

She gave me a twisted and confused look. "Really?"

"Yeah, I'm not feeling so hot."

"Oh." Tess rose and tucked in her chair, motioning to Izabella.

Tess, my best friend in the world, can't handle the thought of someone being ill. It turns her stomach, quite literally. I've told her it's because she's an empath, but she shrugged off that suggestion and responded with it being her weakness, and nothing foo-foo new-age voodoo as she calls it. That girl's got it all wrong. If there was anyone who had more empathy for the world, I challenge them to step up.

From the corner of my eye, I spied Liam shaking hands with the table goers next to us.

"C'mon," I pleaded and kept my head down while pulling out some cash from my wallet and thrusting it in Izabella's direction. "Here." The urge to run to the door overwhelmed me.

Izabella grabbed the money and added her own to it, counting it quickly. "Alright, that should be enough."

Tess stepped over to me. "You're looking a little flushed. Let's get you some air." She looped her arm through mine and yanked back, whispering, "Hey, don't we know that guy?" She was looking right at Liam.

I stammered, unable to make a solid word. It wouldn't take long for her to connect the dots. Her memory was as sharp as a tack. A glance from him to me and back to Liam was all it took. Recognition lit up her face like a neon sign.

"Can we go?" I dropped my gaze to the drink glasses on the table, to the flickering candle in the center and then onto the floor. Long, polished shoes filled my view, and I rolled up the legs of the well-dressed man, over his pants, the classy belt buckle, counted seven buttons on his pin-stripe shirt and met the snicker on his face.

"Camille. What a pleasure to see you here." His voice was smooth, and his tone even smoother.

Tess tugged me back to standing right beside her.

"Liam, these are my friends Tess and Izabella."

He gave each lady a subtle nod. "Pleasure to meet you both."

"Oh, the pleasure is all mine."

I knew what Tess meant as she gave me a look that told me I had a LOT of explaining to do when she got me alone, however, if Liam's ego was anything of size, he probably took it as if it was intended for him.

A sizeable smirk tickled the edge of his lips. Yep, that's exactly what he thought. "Did you enjoy tonight's performance?" he asked us all, but his gaze strayed from my friends.

"I think you play a mean piano." And that was high praise. "I mean, not everyone can play like that, and to put so much soul and feeling into it, it just blew my socks off." I stuck my foot out and waved my bare toes around to prove my point. I should've just shoved my foot into my mouth. It would've been less stupid.

He looked me over. "I see." He turned his dark brown eyes to Tess, and why wouldn't he? She wouldn't have verbal diarrhea. "And you, what did you think?"

"It was amazing. There was this write up in the YEG..." And Tess was off and running, with Izabella adding her thoughts too.

Liam seemed to enjoy the accolades and filled them in on other venues that his band was performing at. Although he took in their comments, I saw his wandering eye.

It did light me up a bit to know I was catching it. And he was a handsome man, so proper and manly. Sexy in an understated way, like a quiet way as if he didn't need to broadcast it to the world. You just knew.

"Well, we really shouldn't hog you from the rest of your fans," Tess said, turning to focus to me. "Camille was starting to feel a little ill, so I should take her home."

"Oh, that's too bad, we were going to go back on in twenty minutes."

"Another time," I said, tightening my grip around Tess's arm and pulling her towards the bar so we could pay our tab. "See you another time."

"First thing Monday morning."

I froze to the carpet. Of course, he would add that.

Tess stopped and for a heartbeat, I worried she would say something. "It was nice meeting you."

"You as well."

Izabella stayed to pay the bill, and Tess and I trudged out to her car without a word. Like a child in trouble, I knew it was coming.

Instead, she started laughing as soon as the doors of her car were closed.

I crossed my arms over my chest. "What?"

She almost snorted she was laughing so hard. "He's your new co-worker, isn't he?"

What? How'd she know? But then, this was Tess. I hung my head. "What's the law of conveniences because I'm about sure I've maxed it out."

She braced her hand on the steering wheel and caught her breath. "Let me see if I can follow this." A sharp inhale filled her lungs. "You met this guy in Mexico at the end of your trip. You came home with him. Trey was at the airport when you two came home, so Will broke up with you. And now you work with him? Did you know he was a teacher when you met him?"

"No. I never asked. What was the point? I wanted my fun and then we were supposed to go our separate ways." I tried to keep it casual sounding. That was the original plan.

She twisted in her seat and gave me a hard look. "Where was Trey when you two landed?"

An older couple walked out of the lounge, arm in

arm, the picture of happiness. They sauntered over to the car behind Tess, and he opened the door for his date and waited until she climbed in.

"The one time the jerk does something romantic and it bites me in the ass. He was waiting for me at the airport waiting area. Complete with a big sign spelling out my name."

Tess's eyes went wide, and she covered the gasp that failed to stay inside her mouth. "Wow."

"Yeah. So, Liam ended it, right there in the airport. Not that we were anything, but he made it pretty clear there would be no future."

Her eyes narrowed and she grabbed my hand. "You like him."

"Nah."

"You do. Look at you. I can hear it in your voice. He's the one that's getting away."

I sighed. "There was nothing between us. We barely kissed. He was just some guy that I hung out with for a couple of days since you were busy." And as soon as the words were out of my mouth, I had regret. Huge stinking piles of it.

Tess crumpled in her seat. "I know. I wasn't a good friend. I'm sorry."

"I'm sorry, I didn't mean for that to come out."

"Sure you didn't. You always say what's on your mind." She started the car when Izabella opened the back door and climbed in.

The ride was rough, and there was so much I wanted to say or ask, but it felt like I'd be sucking up and trying to make amends, so my lips stayed firmly together. Tess had been busy on our trip to Mexico. She had fallen in love. With a real man, not the loser she had been engaged to who cheated on her. I was happy for her, like over the moon thrilled. And if I were being honest with myself, more than a little jealous of it too. I thought it would be a sweet fling, but she gave her heart to the guy, and he did the same. Too bad they lived so far away from each other.

Chapter Seven

I walked to Liam's room first thing on Monday morning. Since he was unfamiliar with the schedule, and Friday had been a wild and crazy day, I thought it would be nice if he had a copy. Our collaboration times were highlighted for him. If he was any other person, I would've been delighted to share time with them, but not Liam. He'd made it pretty clear at the airport that we were done, and all-day Friday, he kept a safe distance.

I rapped my knuckles against the door.

"Come in," he said.

A deep breath of air filled my lungs and I stepped inside his classroom. Keeping my focus on the room, and not the good-looking guy who'd taken my clothing suggestion to heart, I click-clacked my way over to him. Of course, I hadn't taken my own suggestion to heart and was dressed in nicer clothes, all second-hand. Then it wasn't too big a deal if I was someone's personal tissue. They were all wash and wear.

"Good morning, Miss Evans."

There was no point in being rude, although it was tough to tamper down. Something about him made me want to lash out. "When students aren't around, I'm okay with being called Camille."

He nodded and rose from his desk.

Before he could speak, I waved the paper I held in my hands. "I brought you our shared music and gym schedule and marked out when we're expected to get together to plan and implement parts of the curriculum. I can show you what Jesse and I had planned until the end of the year, although I'm always open to fresh new ideas." The paper fluttered out of my hands and onto his desk.

"That's thoughtful of you. Thanks." He stood there, unmoving, staring at me. Was he thinking evil thoughts of me? Wondering why on God's green earth he got transferred to this school? Branding me a cheater?

"You should know, the situation with my boyfriend is very complicated." There I said it. Maybe now he'd stop staring at me with a piteous look on his face.

"I didn't even ask."

"I know, I'm just letting you know. Trey, that's the guy you saw waiting for me, he cheats on me all the time."

Liam sat on the edge of his desk and folded his arms across his chest, but he never took his focus off me. "And you're okay with that?"

For a moment, I narrowed my gaze at him but continued to ramble on. "We're not even boyfriend-girlfriend, although I guess technically, we are. It's so very confusing." My hands flew around me as if they needed agency, and mirroring Liam's stance to stop them flailing about, I folded my arms over my chest and inhaled sharply.

"It doesn't sound that way."

"If you only knew." And if I only understood the damn thing myself. For whatever reason, I was drawn to Trey like a moth to a flame, even though I knew we weren't good for each other. We both knew it. There was nothing spectacular holding us together and yet, when we were lonely and needy, the other was always there. We just understood that about each other. I shook my head and stepped back. The air was getting thick and I was starting to get claustrophobia. "Anyways, I just thought you should know. I hate misunderstandings between people when it's easier to just speak up and tell the truth."

Because I respect you enough to explain the damn thing. What we had in Mexico felt real and genuine. I wished I could say it, but I didn't want to be a fool. That happened enough without me opening my mouth.

"Thank you for sharing, although I'm not sure why you'd tell me. We're only colleagues."

Only colleagues. Any wishes I'd held became dust in the wind. "I don't want things awkward between us."

He blinked a few times and rose. "Fair enough."

"You and me? We weren't even serious." Of all the stupid things to come out of my mouth, because a hint of a strong relationship certainly felt forthcoming. Until Trey showed up.

He walked over to the other side of his desk and clicked on his mouse, bringing up a chart on his smartboard. He grabbed the paper I'd dropped and stabbed it to the board behind him. "Was there anything else you needed, Miss Evans?"

I shook my head, staring at him.

"Then I guess I'll see you," he ran his finger over the chart, "in the gym before recess."

"Yes." I stood there dumbfounded, and after I collected myself, I turned and stalked out of the room.

Shannon waltzed her way over to me. "Good morning. Digging your claws into our new team member?" She glared at me.

"I have no claim on him…" Maybe there had been a chance until my stupid mouth ran itself off. "He's my collaboration partner. You of all people should know the importance of that." Shannon loved her collab time but only the social aspect of it as she was usually found in the staff lounge gossiping rather than planning her week out. Disgraceful really. Her students deserved better.

She waved her manicured hand in my direction. "Good for you, you goodie-two-shoes." She stepped inside his room and drew the door closed, but not all the way. "Liam, darling," she drawled out.

Not one to eavesdrop, I'd normally take off and do my own thing, but something about the way she called out to him rattled my bones and I needed to hear what the tramp said. I leaned against the corridor and opened the door a little wider.

"Shannon, right?"

"That's right." Her voice was sugary.

"What can I help you with?"

"Since you're offering."

I cringed even though I wasn't sure what she was doing, I had my suspicions.

"Miss O'Daughtry, may I be honest with you?"

"Please, it's Shannon, and of course you can." The sweetness rolling off her serpent tongue was enough to give me a mouth full of cavities.

"I'll be straight with you. I don't date colleagues. At all," he said with good measure.

66

I cheered for a heartbeat until I realised that this would also include me. For future reference.

"That's just because you've never met the right one."

"Please stop touching me."

I shuddered and tiptoed over to my class, closing the door. I'd heard enough.

The day came and went, and I was no further ahead. All day long I'd thought about what he'd said, or a lack of what he'd said and how far I'd stuck my foot into my mouth. Maybe I needed to suck up to him, although that was not something I did. Tess always said I was the kind of girl to hit you between the eyes with the truth. Sucking up just wasn't in my DNA. Being nice, sure, but not ass-kissing. I'd watched Tess enough to know she was good at that, which is probably why she got snowballed at work. Thank god she's in a better environment. I'd tried to convince her once to join our school board as an Educational Assistant, but she declined citing that she loved her job just not the people. Something I totally understood, as Shannon and I just did not mix. I felt a smidgen of joy that Liam had shot her down too. Ha-ha.

At dismissal time, I stood outside on the back area

where the parents came to pick up their children. It's a rule that the students need to be released to their designated pickup, especially at the kindergarten level. Liam and I stood there, silently, matching our students with their caregivers.

I had two children still waiting, and Liam had four, which was not uncommon. His class, under Jesse's care, was usually the last for pickup, as either the parents had horrible time management skills or some other strange reason for not being there at dismissal time. I wished parents understood what it felt like to a child to be the last one picked up every day. Speaking from personal experience, it's heartbreaking.

Spotting one of my student's dads, I waved and wished Lily a good afternoon, sending her toward her father. It was great to see dads pick up their children, as it's quite unusual. Lily's nanny always dropped her off and picked her up, but lately, over the past few weeks, it was Mr. Murdoch at the end of the school day.

"Ah, wait," her father said and strutted in my direction. "Can I have a minute with you?" He buttoned his expensive-looking suit jacket.

"Sure," I said. Mentally, I reviewed the last few days with Lily, and nothing stuck out that warranted any formal talking about.

He looked over at Liam and back to me and stepped around to the side of me. "Lily really likes you."

I smiled from the compliment. "I like her too. She's a very smart girl." Where was this conversation going? Lily's sweet upturned face stared up at me.

Mr. Murdoch swallowed, the Adam's Apple bobbing over his Mediterranean dark skin.

The hesitation raised a red flag. When some parents are about to drop bad news, they always open with a compliment. I braced myself.

"She thinks you're very pretty."

I nodded and took a small step backwards, pretending the other child who was still waiting for pickup needed something. I wanted a little distance. I needed a little distance. The conversation just took a weird turn. His harmless flirtatious nature previously was gone, and I was on edge for something a little more personal.

"And I agree with her." His dark eyes locked on me.

Needing more distance, I stepped away further and bumped my back on the door handle. Throwing my focus to the ground, I stared at the square, highly polished shoes inching closer to me.

"Would you be interested in joining us for dinner this Friday night at our place, and then afterward I put Lily and her sisters to bed, we can sit and talk? Maybe Netflix and chill?" His dark eyebrow lifted and with it, a shiver threatened to ripple through my body.

Remain professional. Deep breath. I gathered my sweetest teacher's voice. "Well, Mr. Murdoch, that's a very nice offer but I'm afraid I'll have to decline." *Don't apologize.* Even though I wanted to. My heart hammered in my chest.

"If you have plans, come over afterwards. We don't have to have dinner, just chill." The underlying tone wrapped through his words chilled me, and goose pimples popped all over my arms.

I tore my gaze off his neatly trimmed beard and scanned the area. "No, thank you." Beyond him, I spotted a familiar face – my other student's parent. "Oh, look, Jimmy, there's your mom." I gave little Jimmy's hand a quick squeeze. "Excuse me, Mr. Murdoch." I stepped around him and escorted Jimmy to his mom, taking my time and exchanging pleasantries with her until Mr. Murdoch sauntered passed. He turned to smile in my direction. Twice.

Relief that he was gone, and my students were all picked up, I marched into the school and down the hall to my room. *Note to self – pray that Lily is not the last pick up anymore.* Should I talk with Samantha's—Lily's older sister—teacher and try to get Samantha ready quicker so that both girls were ready to go? Dealing with the unwanted advances from creeps wasn't a chapter in a book I was ready to reread. This was going to end. There had to be an easy solution.

Chapter Eight

fterschool pickups were becoming the worst part of my job, even more than the tension-filled collaboration time with Liam. Unless it was a question about one of the students or something school-related, Liam basically ignored me. I had to find a way to let him go, and I wished it was as easy for me as it had been for him. However, Liam was a problem I could deal with. Mr. Murdoch, on the other hand, was only getting bolder.

He was either second last or last pickup. Where he'd been marginally polite on Tuesday but still a bit flirtatious, he was borderline rude on Wednesday when I politely rejected his dinner invitation. Again. Thankfully Thursday there was no afternoon class; it was the calm before the storm.

Friday afternoon I stood at the door, alone this time, as Liam's students had been picked up quickly. All week long, he'd been putting his foot down about parents being on time, and they responded by actually listening to him. I was impressed and made mental notes to follow his lead. It was too late in the year for me to change, but come a new school year in the fall, I could be tougher.

Spotting Mr. Murdoch rounding the corner, I let go of Lily's hand. "Your dad's here." I hoped she'd run off and save me, but bless the child, she didn't move a muscle.

"That's okay. I'll stay." She reached for my hand and held on tight.

I glanced around. A couple of other teachers mingled about and a few parents too. At least I wasn't out here completely alone. If he got too close, I could holler for help.

"Good afternoon, Miss Evans." His voice gave me the chills, but it was more the underlying sultriness that set off warning bells.

I nodded, looking past his full beard over to the grade five teacher. "Mr. Murdoch." Calmly, trying to maintain as much professionalism as I could muster from the pit of my stomach, I unhooked my hand from Lily's.

Mr. Murdoch hunched down and spoke to his daughter. "Honey, why don't you go play in the park with Samantha? I just need to speak with your teacher a moment."

My heart raced enough to cause pain on my ribcage. Once again, I scanned the immediate area. The crowd was thinning, but I wasn't alone.

"Okay." Like the good girl she was, she skipped off to join her sister and they headed to the park.

"My evening is still free, if you are. I'm making lasagna." He ran his hairy finger over my arm.

The way my stomach churned, throwing up all over him was a strong possibility. The swallow of bile burned as it retraced its path back into my gut. "I'm afraid I have other plans." My voice was firm, and I straightened myself to my full height, which at 5'6" was still way shorter than him. A tuft of chest hair poke through his unbuttoned shirt collar.

"Don't be afraid."

"I'm not afraid." I was terrified but reigned in my quickened breath and hoped to hell that he couldn't tell how fast my heart thudded against my ribs. Is this what a heart attack felt like?

"Good." It was said in the way I'd imagined a tiger would attempt to calm his prey.

He was way too close for my liking and I tried distancing us, but there was nowhere to go. I was already backed against the door. My stomach flipped and my legs tingled. "Excuse me." I spotted a teacher walking towards

74

another set of doors and I needed to join her.

"Where are you going? Why don't you want to go out with me? I'm a nice guy." He pushed his hand up and over my shoulder and braced it on the wall behind me.

"Excuse me." I strengthen my voice. "Trish," I called out.

He grabbed my ass as I ducked out from under the other arm which was about to box in me in. I sprinted away from Mr. Murdoch as fast as possible in heels and raced to catch up with the grade five teacher. "I forgot my keys." It was the best excuse on the fly, but it worked; she let me in through her doors. Without a further glance, I sped to my classroom and closed the door, turning off the lights.

Safe inside, I sat at my desk and kicked off my shoes, eager to lean back and shake some feeling into my feet. Afterschool dismissal wasn't supposed to be like this. It should be something I looked forward to at the end of a busy day, not something to dread. Something needed to change. But how? It wasn't fair to put Lily in another classroom. How her father acted wasn't her fault. Maybe I could trade off with Liam. I'd take care of drop-offs and he'd do the pick-ups. Yeah, that would be perfect.

A knock came from the door and my heart skipped a beat. Who could it be? Not Mr. Murdoch? I listened hard for little voices and hearing none, I pushed it open, hand

75

grasped tightly around the handle in case I needed to slam it shut quickly. "Oh, hey." It was Liam.

His eyes searched my face. "You okay?"

"Oh yeah."

"You're crying."

"What?" I touched my face, under my eyes. Indeed, it was damp. I hadn't been aware that I'd even shed any tears. Turning away from Liam, I kept my voice light. "It's just Friday, and I'm always a little teary when the week ends." Drawing a smile from someplace unknown, I plastered it on and faced him.

He studied me, but he wasn't buying it. His brows furrowed together, and he narrowed his gaze. "That's all?"

"Yep."

A vision of Mr. Murdoch floated into my head, all close and breathy, the remarkable grip from his sizeable hand on my ass. It wasn't romantic in the least and was downright scary. Liam wasn't like that, and I released my breath and my grip, shaking it as I freed it from the handle.

"Can I help you with something?"

"I wanted to apologize for my behaviour this week."

I tipped my head to the side and shifted my weight. The floor wasn't that comfortable with bare feet. "Oh?"

He sighed as if he was choosing his words

carefully. "You understand why I need to keep my distance from you, right?"

Quickly, I scanned the hallway behind him, hoping no other staff member lingered. Liam stepped back and did the same. It was all clear.

"I can't be with someone who doesn't…" He lost his focus on me, and with it, his train of thought. "Anyways, here." He fanned a couple of tickets against my hand. For a brief moment, I enjoyed the soft way his hand brushed against mine. "I have a couple of invites for tomorrow night's performance." A few heartbeats passed, and his gaze returned to my eyes. "We take the stage at nine. I'd really like it if you were there."

My heart pitter-pattered and good vibes coursed through my body. The pub wasn't far from my building and it would be something fun to do. I was sure Tess and Izabella would enjoy going to watch him play. "You'll be there?"

He stepped a little closer, and ran his gaze over me, a smile spreading across his face. "It's my band."

"Oh right. Just checking." I managed a wink, but it probably looked stupid. Sometimes I truly lived up to my hair colour. However, I wasn't thinking straight, and I knew that. The desire to get home and scrub myself free of Mr. Murdoch was a strong need at the moment. A shudder rolled through me.

"You sure you're okay?"

"Just peachy." I darted my gaze to the movement on the right. Just the night custodian. "I really should get going." A quick running step to my desk where I grabbed random papers and shoved them into my bag, clicking out of my computer program. My feet slipped into my heels while I fluffed my hair.

Liam hadn't moved until I got back within scent of him. Damn, he smelled good. He stepped aside, giving me a chance to lock up. Confusion coloured his expression.

I gave him a quick once over. "See you Monday."

"Or tomorrow?" He waved the tickets.

"Right. That's great. Thank you. I'll be there." I popped them out of his hands and dashed to the front door, checking the parking lot security cameras before I headed over to my car.

Safe inside my apartment, I locked the door and slid the chain across. Tears that I'd been holding back on the ten-minute ride home fell fast and furious, but it was time to drown them. I reached into the cabinet for the bottle of whiskey, and filled a glass full, emptying the bottle in the process.

I peered down the stubby neck into it, wondering where the rest had gone? That bottle was damn near full last week. But whatever, the liquor store was only a few blocks away and I had back up alcohol if I needed it. For now, this would burn a solid strip of fire into the pit of my acidic stomach.

Damn, the alcohol went down nice and easy, but what was worse, was seeing the up close and personal face of Mr. Murdoch on the back of my lids as my throat swallowed hard. Fucking jerk. How dare he touch me like that? That suggestive grin on his face. Gag. I wasn't game for a little Netflix… not with the likes of him, that's for sure. Wave after wave of shudders tore through me, and with one, I felt the unmistakable touch across my ass.

"Noooo!" I launched my glass across the empty room. It headed for the patio door, but thankfully it missed its intended target, as that would've been an expensive bill. Instead, it shattered against the wall beside the door, spraying the area with shards of glass and staining the wall with speckles of wet.

My phone rang and I dug it out of my bag. Trey. Someone I'd rather not talk with. The phone rang three times before it finally went to voice mail.

Eight ounces of whiskey on an empty stomach did the job I hoped. Instead of a crystal-clear image of the grabby jerk, the edges blurred inwards until I couldn't make out the details on his face. However, there were moments of clarity and another face started surfacing. A terrifying laugh. Breath heavy with the pungent odor of soured beer. That needed to go away even more, and I ransacked the cabinets for something else to drink. Not the schnapps, not the rum, not even the Malibu. Those all needed something to go with them, and I wanted something hard to pound back immediately.

Ah – fireball. Another whiskey. Cinnamon flavoured. Yum. But where had that come from? My birthday party? Perhaps. There was a lot of alcohol consumed that night, and some even given to me as gifts. Regardless of where it came from, I was happy it was here with me now. Needing a fresh glass, I put a couple of ounces in it and like a sailor on leave, opened my throat and dumped it down.

I held the glass tightly in my hand and blinked hard, focusing on anything else but closing my eyes. The faucet on the sink. The bills piled high above the bread box. My bag at the front door. I blinked. Once. Twice. Nothing was staying put. Everything swayed from side to side. Damn. At least I wasn't seeing that horrid face anymore.

A knock sounded on the door, and heart dropping

into my stomach, I half expected the door to suddenly open. But it didn't.

Trey's voice muffled through the door. "I know you're home. I saw your car downstairs. You can't ignore me forever. Can I come in?"

Swaggering over to the door, I stopped beside it, bracing myself against the counter. I blinked some more and tried to focus on the doorknob, but I couldn't get it to turn. "It's slippery."

"What's slippery?"

"The door."

"Have you been drinking?"

"Maybe. But just a little." My vision blacked out for a quick sec. "I just got home." My hand finally wrapped around the knob and I yanked it open, but the chain caught it. "It's stuck," I said defeated. Really though, there wasn't any point in helping it. If I gave it enough time it would open itself. Damn thing couldn't stay still.

"Cammy, close the door and slide the chain off."

"No." *Not tonight.*

"No?" His voice pitched. "Let me in."

My forehead banged into the side of the door and I winced. "It's not good in here." Mr. Murdoch resumed his ghostly appearance. That icy cold voice of his repeating over and over how lovely it would be if I joined him for supper. The thought of Netflixing and chilling…

"Exactly why I need you to let me in."

Tears burst from me, my breathing raced, and my voice cracked. "I can't, Trey. It's not safe."

"What do you mean it's not safe? Cammy, let me in." His voice cracked and a steely look clouded his face.

I slumped to the floor and peered at him through the crack. "He's everywhere."

"Who?"

"I can't unsee him. I can't unfeel him. I don't want to smell him anymore."

"Cammy, you're scaring the hell out of me." He knelt on to the floor and pushed his fingers through the inch of space between the door and the frame in a desperate attempt to touch me. "Please, let me in. Let me help you."

I pulled away further, slouching against the wall. My head rolled to the side and I stared at him weakly. "No one can help me."

Chapter Nine

A shudder violently rippled through me and I opened my eyes. I blinked and took in my surroundings. I was sitting on the floor beside the door, which was cracked open, with Trey on the other side. My gaze followed up the door to see that the chain was still in place, and that's what was supporting a sleeping Trey.

"Hey," I whispered through the door. He wasn't close enough to touch.

I pushed myself to a standing position and braced myself against the wall as my head spun around. Putting my weight into the door, I managed to close it enough to slip the chain free and open it.

Trey moved, slowly at first and then a burst of speed took over. He scrambled onto his feet. "Cammy."

I felt sheepish and stared at his shoes. "Hey. The couch is much comfier if you want to sleep."

"I wasn't sleeping." A large yawn escaped him. "Much."

My voice fell. "You didn't have to stay."

"Right. Because I was going to leave when you were like that. I'm many things, but I'm not a loser."

I nodded at the truth and opened the door further. "Before you ask, it's closed, okay?"

"But?"

"It's not up for discussion." I shut and re-chained the door after he came in. "But thank you. I appreciate you staying out in the hallway."

He shrugged and rubbed his eyes again. "S'all good. Mrs. Tautenbaum must've thought we had a fight or something. I'm sure I provided some juicy gossip at her group gathering of the elderly."

I laughed. Mrs. Tautenbaum was at least eighty, but spry as can be. She and a group of other widows met weekly for a game of cards on Friday night. I can only imagine the hushed voices and whisperings that went on as they passed my door on their way to hers. Mrs. Tautenbaum thought Trey lived with me, and I was on the end of her constant tsking quite a bit. Naturally, I avoided the old bat every chance I got.

Trey ambled into the living room and stopped. "What the hell?"

Following behind him, I too stopped and stared. A bright brown stain hung on the wall near the patio door and shards of glass were everywhere.

"Don't sit on the couch," I said to Trey.

A look of confusion filled his face when he turned to me. "What the hell happened?"

"Not up for discussion." The mess was everywhere, and I wondered how far-reaching the tiniest piece of glass flew? My vacuuming job would need to be superior when I tackled it. But it was after midnight, so it wasn't going to happen tonight. "Come on." I grabbed Trey's hand. "Let's go to bed."

I wasn't in a sexy mood, but I did want to stretch out. Kinks ran rampant through my body.

Still dressed in my skirt and blouse, I climbed under the covers and rested my heavy head on my double-stacked pillows. Trey shook out of his jeans, leaving on his boxers and tee-shirt, and slipped in behind me. "Is it safe to snuggle?"

"You're good." Secure and feeling safe under his arm, I pushed my back into his chest.

An alarm, somewhat muted, woke us the next morning. Trey scrambled out of bed and dug in his jeans for the source of the noise. "Damn, I'm going to be late." He turned the alarm off and rushed to the door. "Sorry."

"Don't be." I climbed out of bed looking as wrinkled as I felt and followed him down the hall. "What time are you done tonight?"

"Six."

"I have an extra ticket for a jazzy band show. Want to join me?" I should've asked the ladies first since Liam had suggested it for her. But after everything he did for me last night...

"Since when are you into jazz?"

"It's a co-worker. He plays the piano for the band. Show's at eight."

Trey's eyes darted between my left and right one, as if he was trying to sort out in his mind what exactly was going on in mine. "Okay."

"Are you sure? You don't sound it."

"I'm intrigued. I'll pick you up at 7:30?"

"Fine."

The chain slid free from its holding and Trey planted a quick kiss on my cheek. "Later."

I sighed as I closed and locked the door. Leaning against it, I stared out blankly. It was time to clean up my mess. Only problem was, I didn't know where to start.

Trey and I parked a block away from the venue, located off the hip Whyte Ave.

I hesitated as we approached the lounge, taking in the signage at the door. People mingled around us and entered; however, I couldn't make my feet move. They were frozen in cement. What would Liam think if he spotted me here with Trey? Likely, it would solidify that there would be no future between us, something I wanted, even if right now, Liam was a no-go on it.

"You coming in?" Trey stood there, hands in his jean pockets.

At least we were both the same level of casual. I wore a simple dress, like something I'd wear to school and not a bar like the last time. "I don't know." I tossed my gaze to the bay window. I sighed, worry running through me faster than my pounding heartbeat. Liam was at the forefront of my thoughts. I'd tried to explain that Trey and I aren't really boyfriend and girlfriend, but I'm not sure I was convincing. After last night, I wasn't even convinced myself.

"It'll be fine. Nothing's going to happen here. It's a jazz lounge."

Well, if that wasn't a ringing endorsement but laughed because it wasn't the venue that worried me.

However, I stepped inside and took the lead, presenting the tickets to the doorman.

"Ah, your table is right this way." He escorted us to an area off to the side, but with an easy line of sight to the piano. Clever.

Trey shrugged out of his jean jacket and wrapped it around the chair.

Flagging down a server, he ordered himself an ice-cold beer, and asked what I wanted.

Clarity. But instead of opening my mouth, I ordered a whiskey neat. "Can I ask you something?" I stared at the candle in the center of our table, mesmerized by the way the flickering highlighted some of the decorative beads around it but not the others.

Trey moved his chair closer and tilted his head down. "What's up?"

"Tonight... are we here as just friends?"

His eyes narrowed and he reached out to touch my arm, but for whatever reason stopped and pulled back. "What do you mean?"

"Can we just be friends?" I didn't want Liam to think that something was going on between Trey and me, when there wasn't. If he stopped by our table, I needed it clear that Trey and I were not romantically linked.

Trey huffed and ran his hands through his hair.

They fell over his brows in a relaxed way. I envied his hair. "Let me ask you something."

"Okay." My breath threatened to choke me.

"Did we come together?"

I chuckled and released my air. "Of course, we live in the same building. It would've been crazy to have taken two vehicles and paid twice for parking."

"Fair enough." Trey fiddled with his cloth napkin. "Would you consider this a date?"

"Umm…" I hadn't, until he said it. But it wasn't a date-date, just two people going out to watch a live band. Tess and I did this last week and it wasn't considered a date.

His blue eyes connected with mine and he swallowed. "Did we break up somewhere and I missed the memo?"

Like a deer in the headlights, I couldn't move, and my brain went blank.

"Are we still a couple, Cammy?"

I stared into his eyes. It was a hard question to hear and probably a harder question to ask. Trey wasn't known for stepping up to the plate. I wasn't sure what the answer should be. There were many times when I honestly thought we weren't a couple, with all the cheating going on, and yet when it came down to something tough, he was there without fail. I sighed and wrapped my arms around my chest to hold myself together.

"I haven't given up on you. Have you given up on me?" Trey ran a finger over my arm and a violent shudder coursed through me along with an image of Mr. Murdoch instantly surfacing in my head.

"STOP."

He pulled back like a snapped elastic.

It wasn't meant for Trey, but for that horrid picture of an awful man I couldn't shake out of my head. I twitched in my seat and cupped my head in my hands, breathing sharply through intense chest pain.

"What the hell happened yesterday?"

"I don't want to talk about it." Goosebumps covered my arm and the image planted itself on the forefront of my brain. I resumed my staring at the candle flickers, trying desperately to burn away the ghosted picture. It also calmed my breathing.

Trey stretched out for a few heartbeats and sipped from his mug of beer.

I grabbed my drink and devoured the taste. Glass empty, I flagged down our server.

"Can I help you?" He stood attentively beside Trey.

"I need another, please." I nodded at the glass I

gripped between my fingers.

Trey straightened up. "No, she doesn't. Just bring her a large water, please."

The waiter looked at him, at me and once again to Trey.

"Honestly, she's fine with the water." He dismissed the server with a wave.

I turned my head and shot a set of daggers at him. *Jerk. I needed that. Badly.* The dancing flame re-grabbed my focus, but my wandering thoughts became fixated on wanting to get home and have a drink there. About to stand and leave, our table got bumped.

The band wiggled their way through the tables and crowds, taking their respective spots on stage. Liam sat down on his piano bench and rifled through the stacked music sheets. He scanned the crowd and rested his gaze on me. He looked at Trey and he shook his head. Back in Mexico, he had been interested in me, but after last weekend, maybe he had taken a liking to Tess, who was enthusiastic about his being in a band. Was he disappointed she wasn't here with me? Or was it the man on my left that caused him to look rejected?

Chapter Ten

*M*onday rolled around faster than it normally would. Weekends were never long enough, especially when you don't remember much of what happened. The fault lays with Jack. Jack Daniels. At least I didn't break another glass over the remainder of the weekend.

Hungover, twenty-one screaming five-year-olds were not a pleasant experience.

"Hey." Liam knocked on my door and entered, staying near the entrance.

One of my students ran over and hugged him.

"Hi, Jasmine," he said, patting her on the back. After she hopped over to her table, he looked at me. "I'm in desperate need of help. My smartboard blanked right in the middle of a story."

"Oh sure. Gimme a sec." I sent down one of the

magnetic letters I was helping a student with as I rose. "Mrs. Barrie, I'll be right back."

Mrs. Barrie was my assistant, and a damn fine one. Old enough to be my mother, but sweeter than apple pie. The students loved her, and I adored her. I wish there was enough money in the school budget to keep her full-time, but as it was, I only got her in the mornings.

I glanced at the clock on the wall. "Actually Mrs. Barrie, if you could get them ready for recess, that would be great." I followed Liam's fine form across the hall to his room. "What happened?"

"Hi, Miss Evans," one of the students sang out.

I high fived him and followed Mr. Donaldson over to his desk.

The computer screen was blank too. "The video was playing and all of a sudden, the screen flickered, and went black. I managed to figure out that it had been disconnected from the power supply somehow, but I can't get it to work even after plugging it back in."

"Hmm..." I gave Liam a once over. He was definitely uptight and worried, pacing between students. "I'm sure it's an easy fix." Pulling his chair in, I sat and started typing, giving the occasional glance to the smartboard at the front of the class. Nothing appeared. No prompts or icons. I tried out a couple of other tricks I kept up my sleeves, also to no avail.

"See what I mean?"

"I do." My fingers continued clicking. I wasn't quitting just yet. "That was a great show on Saturday. Thanks again for the tickets."

He stopped his wandering and sat at one of the tiny tables with a student. Sitting there, with his legs stuck out to the side, made him seem even taller than normal. The tables weren't designed for a six-foot-tall man. It was rather endearing to see him like that. "You and your boyfriend enjoyed it?"

The little girl sitting at the table looked over at me. "You have a boyfriend?" She practically squealed in delight. "I have one too. His name is Brandon and he lives down the street from me." She was too cute in how she went on about him.

When she finished, I answered Liam's question. "Yes, actually Trey quite enjoyed it. I told him to close his eyes and feel the music. It gives it an entirely different experience."

"Wow." Liam doodled on the paper with his student.

"My friend, the one that came with me last time, she suggested that. Her boyfriend's going blind and she has an appreciation for seeing things in a new light. So to speak." I clicked on the keyboard that refused to cooperate. Why the hell was the smartboard not responding to my commands and prompts? What I really wanted to do was hit it a few times as that always worked on mine. Our budget didn't allow for upgrades and most of the time our equipment was several years old and sometimes a good smack did wonders. I stood under the projector and stared up. "Ryan, can I borrow your chair?"

The little boy pushed his chair over to me.

I kicked out of my heels and climbed up, reaching high above me. My shirt raised to bare my midriff, and from the corner of my eye I spotted Liam staring. I won't lie, I enjoyed that.

"Why does this need to be so high?"

The reset button I needed was on the top of the machine because why wouldn't it be? The unit itself was suspended from the ceiling so logically, having the button in an impossible place was smart thinking. I reached my hand up and over, feeling for it. Sensing it beneath my finger, I gave it a hard push and reset the projector.

Liam had moved to stand beside me. "Careful there."

I was gazing down on him and looked deep into his eyes as the board flickered beside us with the start-up menu.

The recess bell rang, and I nearly jumped off my tiny chair in surprise.

Liam braced his hands on my hips before I lost my balance and toppled off. He steadied me while the little ones rushed out of the classroom, talking loudly. The volume level decreased dramatically and, in a heartbeat, it was just the two of us, standing as if we didn't have a care in the world. He looked up at me, a longing in his dark browns while they lingered on my face.

I wanted to cup my hands around his cheeks and lean down to place a sweet kiss on his lips, the way I had in Mexico, but I sensed a hint of hesitation from him.

The computer blasted its bleeps and sounds as the system finished rebooting, totally killing the first pleasant vibe we'd had with each other since he started here.

"Let me help you down." He offered his hand of which I graciously accepted, and I stepped off the chair.

As quickly as the sensations started, they ended. With my feet firmly planted on the carpet, he backed away and stared at the computer screen. He clicked on the start-up and the board roared to life.

"It's working, thanks."

"My pleasure." And for a few heartbeats, it really was. A girl could get used to this. I stood there, waiting for something to happen. For him to say anything more but when nothing occurred I turned and dejected, went to my classroom to tidy up.

The worst part of my day raced to greet me—afternoon dismissal. Students milled around laughing and playing their made-up game while parents chattered.

"So…" Liam started and paused as he handed off one of his students. "I was wondering…" He inhaled sharply. "It goes against everything in me, but I'm curious…" He handed off another of his students while my five students who had yet to be picked up hung around me. "If you have dinner plans."

Wow. A flight of butterflies took flight. I'd been hoping for him to make a move. It was a good sign.

"Just as colleagues though."

And my heart just crushed out each one of the little bugs. Of course, it would have to be that way. He knew I was with Trey, in our weird little relationship.

One of my parents arrived and I sent off my student.

"I… don't have dinner plans." I handed off another student. Liam's had all picked up, lucky dog.

"Great. Want to meet at Monty's for five? I have a few things I need to do beforehand."

"Five works." The restaurant was a couple of blocks from here. A total dive on the outside, but they made the best fire-baked pizza ever, so it made up for the stylish exterior.

"See you there." I still had three more students, one of whom was Lily. As each student went home with a parent or guardian, only Lily remained. It was later than usual, and my heartbeat picked up its pace. "Come on, Lily. I'll take you to the office." No way was I being stuck out there alone. With him, the Master Creeper. We headed through a set of doors and made our way toward the office where I watched out the front doors, waiting. At least here, there were cameras.

A sigh of sweet relief rolled out of me when I spotted Lily's nanny. Opening the front door, I called out her name and waved her over.

Edalyn walked over and took Lily's hand without a word.

"See you tomorrow," I said. It was an odd exchange, but I chalked it up to her being flustered for being late. Maybe she'd get in trouble for that when she got home, I didn't know. Whatever, at least I didn't have to deal with him.

I strolled down the quiet hall to my class thinking about tonight's dinner non-date with Liam. Should I go home and change? Or would that look like I'm trying too hard? There wasn't anything wrong with my pants and ruffled sleeved shirt, but I did want to make a good impression. Show him that I wasn't a total write-off. Maybe I'd be best to let my hair down and freshen up and leave it at that.

Liam's door was closed, and the lights were turned off. It seemed as though he'd already taken off. Mind you, if he had to run home and come back to this part of the city, it would be nearly an hour round trip, and we were meeting in ninety minutes. Oh well. We could chat over dinner.

I had a bunch of Easter items I needed to prepare for the week, and I'd been given the gift of time. Walking into the room, I put on some Garth Brooks and dug around in my tiny closet for the bunny-themed items I'd grabbed on sale last year. I backed out of the closet, right into the hard wall of Liam. "Changed your mind about supper?"

His arms wrapped tightly around me and before he spoke, I knew it wasn't Liam. The smell was different, the way his breath singed the nape of my neck. My heart pounded against his hairy arms. Oh shit. Mr. Murdoch. I pushed against him, but I couldn't break free of his hold. He had me pinned. "You can struggle all you want, but I'm stronger than you." His breath warmed my skin but gave me goosebumps. With intense strength, he lifted me and carried me deeper into my own classroom.

"What do you want?" I asked, hoping my voice

was not the crackly nervous I felt coursing through my body at breakneck speeds.

"Why you, of course. Except you keep rejecting me." He set me down, spun me around, and slammed me into the wall. My head connected with one of the pushpins holding a child's artwork.

"I have a boyfriend." My breath caught on a lump in my throat. "So, it wasn't personal."

"Bullshit." His face was close enough to mine; his bottom lip had a crazy twitch as his eyes darkened. His hand grabbed my wrist, locking around as he twisted it behind my back.

Pain shot through my right arm, and a feeling of doom washed over me. This wasn't going to end well, and every fiber in my body knew that. I'd been down this road before.

With his other hand, he gripped my left wrist and joined it with my right, his hold on my hands strong enough to crush the bones. He squeezed without mercy. His full body pushed against mine and I turned my head away. I couldn't bear to see the sight in his eyes, it wasn't joy, it wasn't fear either. More like a dominance. His free hand gripped my jaw and twisted my face toward him.

In a heartbeat, his mouth claimed mine, forcing his tongue against my teeth I refused to open. His hand squeezed harder and instinctively, my jaw slackened. He used that to his advantage and thrust himself deeper inside my mouth. It was disgusting and I fought off the gagging sensation. His free hand ran down my neck and slowly over my chest, cupping and squeezing that which was not his.

I couldn't speak.

I couldn't say no.

His strong thigh pushed between mine, and he rubbed against me. The urge to throw up was growing, but I knew it would only make things worse. I fought that buildup as hard as I could, imagining myself far away. Someplace warm. Where the sun always shone, and the breeze held the scent of fresh flowers. Mexico. Where Liam and I had met, and all was perfect and happy.

My zoning out skills were getting better, as I heard Liam's voice on the breeze. It was music to my ears, and I imagined him in his white polo shirt and green shorts, his hair damp from a quick swim in the pool. Slicks of water and beads ran along the nape of his tanned neck.

"Hey." A voice called out.

Chapter Eleven

I opened my eyes in a flash. Liam stood at the entrance to my class with the most intense look I've ever witnessed. Sweet relief blanketed me. Never have I enjoyed being interrupted so much.

"Just having a little fun with my girlfriend," Mr. Murdoch said, pulling his hand away from between my legs and releasing my pinned hands. "Right, honey?" He gave me another serpent kiss, his tongue flickering out between his lips. His hand gave my boob another squeeze.

"You're not her boyfriend, and even if you were, she doesn't look one bit comfortable." Liam's gaze darted over to me but returned to Mr. Murdoch with steely determination. "I suggest you step away from her right now." He pulled out his cell phone. The camera clicked.

Mr. Murdoch stepped back, and a cold draft blew between us. There was enough distance that I slipped behind him and wobbled over to my desk, keeping my eyes trained on my jacket hanging on the back of my chair.

A moment later, our body-building custodian Mr. Wentworth and my principal, Mr. Saunders, both appeared at the doorway to my classroom. Mr. Murdoch was trapped. How they knew to come was beyond me.

"Can you two please watch this scum in here until the police arrive? He just assaulted Miss Evans."

"Take her to my office," Mr. Saunders said. "We'll take care of this." He nudged the custodian.

Mr. Wentworth, who was rumoured to have benched 350 just recently, stood at the entrance with his arms crossed over his chest. If you didn't know him, you'd be fearful of the 6'3" giant. His arms were thicker than my thighs. I knew he was a gentleman and we'd always gotten along famously. However, the anger in his expression told me he wasn't to be trifled with. He had no fear of the bad guy in the room and stood face to face with him.

"Come on," Liam said to me. "Get your things. We're going to Saunders room."

Hands shaking, I grabbed my jacket, twice, and retrieved my purse from the bottom desk drawer and not looking in Mr. Murdoch's direction, I followed Liam out of the room.

"Are you okay?" His voice was calm and soothing;

the total opposite of what I was feeling.

"I'm fine." I marched down the hall, bile rising higher and higher the further away I got and there was no way I was going to make to Saunder's office without a visit to a restroom.

Without asking permission, I dipped into the girl's washroom and opened the first stall door, dropping to my knees. Until my stomach was completely devoid of its contents, I stayed there. The coldest shiver rippled through me, and a bead of sweat broke out under my arms and on the backs of my knees.

Physically empty, I flushed and walked over to the child-sized sink, scrubbing my hands and scratching at the skin with my nails until they were red and raw. I filled my mouth with cool handfuls of water and swished and sip. Righting myself, I took a glance at myself. I looked worse than the nights at the bar when I'd had too much to drink. The colour of my skin was akin to death, even with makeup on. I gave my hair a quick fluffing, not that it helped. I was still a mess.

Tossing my shoulders back and lifting my head, I marched out of the bathroom to an exasperated Liam who was pocketing his phone and glancing down the hall.

"Are you okay?"

"Better, thanks."

He lifted his hand as if he wanted to rest it on my back, but it dropped to his side.

Figures. Once people think you've been assaulted in some way, they refrain from touching you. It's one of the reasons I've never said anything to anyone about my past. I didn't need to be treated like I was a leper or something.

"I called the police. They're on their way."

I nodded and led the way to Saunder's office, passed the front doors and to the office tucked into the corner. With its boxy design and furnishings, his private space was not very comfortable or inviting. Still, I took a seat in one of the three chairs and waited.

Going over the past few weeks, I went over every detail of every conversation I'd had with Mr. Murdoch. In no way had I led him on. Not once. He wasn't my type. I hadn't responded to his flirts. I never batted my eyelashes. I couldn't recall a single thing I did that would make him think I wanted that kind of contact with him. But it wouldn't matter. He was male, and I was female. It would somehow be my fault.

I spotted a jar of mints on Saunder's desk and helped myself. If it was one thing I needed to do immediately, it was rid myself of the foul taste still lingering in my mouth.

Liam knocked on the door and escorted the officer in. "I'll leave you two to talk." He closed the door and disappeared.

The officer removed his hat and tucked it under his arm. "I'm Officer Tang, and I'd like to get your statement."

I huffed and crossed my legs as I leaned forward. "I'll save you time. I'm not giving one."

He just stood there. "Ma'am, we can't hold him without a reason."

"It doesn't matter." I stood but kept my distance from the policeman. "I can tell you the truth about what happened and give you all the details." A shudder ran through me, igniting a surge of adrenaline. "You'll hold him or whatever, and he'll get released, if he even got held. Nothing will happen to him. He won't serve jail time, and if by some fluke, he was held and needed sentencing, *I* would be the one put through the wringer and dragged through the mud." I pointed at my chest. "*My* reputation would be tarnished, and *I'd* be the one painted poorly. Not him. So, you know what, Officer Tang, I'll just refuse to co-operate." I marched to the door, leaving him behind.

Chapter Twelve

L iam lingered around the main entrance.

"I'm going home," I told him as I walked toward him.

Our secretary, who was still working, watched me go by. I hated that I was the focus of this. Other things I didn't mind, but something of this nature, it was unnerving being studied. It was almost like a neon sign flashing "Damaged Goods".

"That was quick." Liam's eyes flickered to the office where presumably Officer Tang still stood. "You gave your statement already? Are they going to arrest him and charge him? Is he spending the night in jail?"

"I'm done." My gaze fell to the floor and my voice fell to a whisper.

"Well, what did they say? Can the jerk be refused entrance to the school?"

"I said I'm done." My voice regained its strength and I flashed a glance to his face. It dropped with sadness. "Sorry, I'm cancelling our supper date tonight." I'd really been looking forward to going. But all I wanted right now was to go home and scrub.

Liam slowly nodded. "Yeah, understandable. Let me drive you home."

It was sweet to suggest, but I was more than capable of getting myself home. "I'll be fine."

"Honestly. I insist." He pulled himself up to his full height and his voice began to firm but not to an intimidating level.

"If you wanted to see my place, all you had to do was ask." I raised a brow at him, faking a smile.

He didn't return it. "This is hardly the time or place."

"It's all I've got." I shrugged.

"It's so not." He opened the door and I went by him.

My car was still parked in its stall, but I wonder if it should be moved? Did Mr. Murdoch know what I drove? How worried should I be that he would stalk me? What would've happened if he'd followed me home and forced his way into my apartment? A nasty thought and a repulsive feeling washed over me and squeezed my soul. I knew exactly what could've happened—there would've been no interruptions. Breath froze inside my lungs, and it wasn't even that cold out. My heart skipped a beat and I braced myself against a car while I tried to gain control over my body.

"Camille?"

My legs weakened, my heart rate increased tenfold and my stomach tightened and twisted to the point I tasted bile in the back of my throat. I shivered and pulled myself deeper inside my thin jacket.

"Come on." He hesitated when reaching for my hand.

I slumped down the side of the car until my butt hit the asphalt.

"Not here." He extended his hand. "Please?"

It was the pleading in his voice that rumbled me to my senses. I linked my fingers into his and stood. "I just need to catch my breath."

"You're freezing. My car is just over there."

I nodded quickly and inhaled a deep breath. Things inside me were starting to settle down.

Like a perfect gentleman, he opened the passenger door and I slipped into the interior. He sat on his side and touched the iPad screen between us, sending a blast of heat focused in my direction.

"What kind of car is this?" There was no dash, no odometer, nothing like you'd see inside a typical car. Everything was on the iPad screen, which he was tapping his finger on.

"Tesla, model 3."

It meant nothing to me, but it was unlike anything I'd ever seen. It was futuristic.

"It's an electric car. I do a lot of driving, and this is much cheaper. I need your address, please."

"Okay." I gave it to him which he typed into the computer. A map appeared and plotted out the quickest route.

"Away we go." The car started moving.

"It's on?" There wasn't a sound at all. My car, a little beater, was loud enough most of the people in my building knew when I'd fired it up.

He smiled. "Sure is."

It was fascinating watching the screen while he drove. He pointed out a bunch of features I'm sure a car person would've drooled over. They meant nothing to me, but it was a welcome distraction and for the ten-minute drive, it kept me from going too deep into my head. Plus, Liam was excited to share his technology.

He pulled into the parking lot of my building.

"I'm afraid there's no underground parking, but

you can park in my stall. I'm the first on the left." I pointed it out to him. "No one parks beside me." It was a sweet parking spot. No door dings. Not that it mattered on my beater, but it would on a nice car like this.

We ascended two flights of stairs to my level. I half expected to see Trey since he usually popped by Monday nights before he headed to work. Guess since I was stuck at work longer than I wanted to be, he must've left.

I put my key into the lock. "Just a heads up. It's not a fancy apartment." Rent ate over 60% of my income but at least it included all my utilities and had in-suite laundry – a huge perk. There was also a pool on the opposite side of the grounds available, but it had too much chlorine and nearly burned my skin last time I swam there.

"I promise not to look and take notes."

I opened the door; thankful I'd cleaned up after breakfast. My place wasn't perfect but at least it was clean. Trey's, on the other hand, was total opposite, which was why we always shacked at my place.

I dropped my purse into the closet and hung my jacket. "Can I get you anything to drink?"

"No, thank you."

"Hang your coat there, if you like. My place is pretty self-serving. If there's something you want, go get it."

"I like that philosophy." Liam stepped into the living room, leaving me to my own devices in the kitchen.

"Well, I'm not much of a hostess, so it's better for you this way." I reached into the cupboard and retrieved a glass and a new, unopened bottle of whiskey. I broke the seal on the label and poured myself half a glass, taking a solid gulp before refilling and joining Liam in my living room.

He sat on one side of the couch, a lovely floral antique from the likes of Grandma's house, hidden beneath a washable king-sized fitted sheet that wrapped perfectly around it. She didn't need it when she moved into the nursing home and I did. It worked out for both of us.

"How long have you been here?"

The lack of pictures on the wall, boxes tucked into the corner, and the sparsely decorated interior would say less than a month. "Two years." I just wasn't into decorating and I didn't have the wonderful family to see all the time to snap pictures at happy locations and events and hang those up. My life was pretty much me, Tess, Izabella and a couple of university ladies.

"Nice."

"You're just being polite." I took another gulp, feeling the burn as I let it slide down my throat. It was strong but should disinfect my mouth from the vileness of

Mr. Murdoch. I took another taste and swished it around my mouth before swallowing it. If I poured it over my eyes, would it burn away the image? Could I pour it over my boob, and have it wash away the feeling that he was still squeezing it? What about between my legs? I shuddered and crossed them tightly.

"What are you drinking?" He took it out of my hands and gave it a sniff.

"Whiskey. It's killing the germs in my mouth. Help yourself if you want. It's on the counter."

His head tipped to the side and he stared at me. "I don't think liquor will solve anything."

"It's a start." I yanked the glass from his hand and dumped the rest into my mouth.

Liam leaned forward and rested his forearms on his thighs. "Do you want to talk about it?"

"There's nothing to talk about."

"I saw him with–"

"I said there's nothing to talk about." The urge to throw the glass overwhelmed me. Instead of tossing it, I set it down and squeezed my hands into tight fists. My eyes slammed shut and every muscle in my body tensed. One-two-three. I inhaled and relaxed my shoulders, allowing my arms to slacken. Finally, I opened my eyes.

It didn't work. I still saw that awful face, the

unpleasant tickling of beard hairs on my chin and the ghostly sensations of him touching me. Tears built in my eyes and before I'd let them be seen, another drink called out my name and I jumped and headed to the kitchen.

The liquid splashed as I poured it in; I was unable to keep my hand steady. A knock came from the door, and I jumped and screamed causing my tears to break from their holds and embarrass me as they fell down my face.

Liam was suddenly at one end of the galley kitchen, his eyes focused hard on the drinking glass.

The knock came again.

"Cammy, it's me."

Trey.

I opened the door, this time without the chain on. "Hey."

One look was all he took, and he nodded for me to open the door further. "What's going on?"

"It's okay."

"The hell it is." He eyed the liquor on the counter and the man at the other end of it. "Who are you?"

"William."

Trey's eyes narrowed. "You're that guy from the airport." Trey missed that Liam was also part of the band we listened to. He only had eyes for the lead singer and didn't notice that Liam was also part of the ensemble.

"You're the boyfriend?"

Trey's eyes fell to me as if he expected me to answer. But what was the right answer? "Why are you crying?"

"Just a bad day at work."

"Again?" Trey wiped away my tears with his finger. "What's going on? You've had more bad days than good lately."

I turned and braced myself against the counter. Trey on one side of me, Liam on the other but more than an arm's length away. And I wanted Liam closer. "It's okay. Don't worry about me."

"Cammy, I can worry about you if I want."

He put his hand on my back and I cringed from the weight of it, arching myself away. Tears fell from my face in a silent stream, creating a puddle on the counter. I had no reason to fear Trey, he'd never hurt me, and yet, it was instinctual to move away from the touch.

"Shouldn't you get off to work? You're going to be late." I sniffed but kept my head solidly between my arms. There was no reason for me to move. "I promise I'm fine."

"I'm not believing that. I know you better."

"You need to go. I won't have you be late on my account."

"I'm worried about you. Is it him?"

"Him who?"

Trey leaned closer, his breath warming my ear. "Your new friend." It made the hairs on the back of my neck stand at attention and I hated that Murdoch suddenly had that power to make my body respond negatively and the bastard wasn't even here.

"No, Liam's been nothing but sweet." I tipped my head up and looked Trey in the eyes. "I'll be fine. I am fine. Honestly."

There was a lot of hesitation but finally, he backed away and went to the door. "Call or text me if you need anything. I can be here in twenty minutes."

"I'm fine." Thankfully, the alcohol was starting to take effect. Soon I'd be numb and wouldn't feel anything. Sweet relief was within my grasp.

He leaned in to kiss me, and I subtly shook my head. "Take care of her," he said to Liam as I closed the door.

"I'm trying. Believe me."

Chapter Thirteen

*L*iam ordered a large pepperoni pizza while I excused myself and went to take a shower. I scrubbed and scoured and soaped and lathered but no matter what I did, Murdoch's imprint was everywhere. How did I remove the stench the last time the whole thing happened? Why couldn't I remember what I'd done? Or maybe I'd been so good at disassociating from it that it felt like more of a bad dream than an actual traumatizing event. Whatever it was, I wished my attempts worked now. Even the alcohol was limited in its effectiveness. Touching myself felt weird and as much as I wanted to scrub everything clean, all I did was give everything a surface washing.

I redressed and stared at the plethora of makeup. Should I bother? Liam had said he didn't date co-workers, and after what went down today, I wouldn't even make the list if we weren't. But then I'd go out to the living room looking raw and naked, and I wasn't ready for that. The makeup went on, and I ran a brush through my hair, pinning it into a clip.

"Feeling a bit better?" Liam asked as I padded into the living room, the scent of fresh pizza hung in the air and my stomach growled in response to the greasy smell.

"To be honest, no." I went to grab plates but noticed the order came with paper plates. What a nice surprise. No dishes. I put a piece of pizza on my plate and dabbed at it with my napkin.

"I'm sorry."

"Pepperoni's good."

Liam shifted in his seat and turned to face me. "Not about that. About today. The incident at school."

I briefly closed my eyes and opened them in a flash when the nasty image of the asshole appeared. "It's not your fault."

He sighed and added a slice to his paper plate. "I know you don't want to talk about what happened, but I do have a couple of questions."

I stopped mid-chew and stared at the pizza box.

Liam carried on. No matter what I did or how I'd earlier said I didn't want to talk about it. "So, this guy, which student is his?"

Whew. That was an acceptable question. I

swallowed down a lump of food and wiped my mouth. "Lily."

"Perfect. I'll take over her dismissal, if the bastard has the balls to even show his face around the school." He devoured his piece in record time. Guess he was hungry. Although, I think lions eat their prey with a little more enjoyment.

"Thank you. I appreciate that."

"Although we should look into having her moved to another school. Can we do that?"

I had no idea. This was new to me. I didn't know what the rules stated as far as Mr. Murdoch's pickup or if he would be barred from entering the school grounds, which would be totally okay by me. If I never had to see him again, it would still be too soon. However… "That's not fair to Lily though."

"No, it's not, but we can't risk having him around. You deserve to be safe."

My stomach turned to lead, and the food just added to the weight.

"We should talk to the principal tomorrow and find out what we can and can't do. What he did was wrong, so wrong, and well, we don't have to be nice in return." He slapped another slice on his plate.

"Excuse me." I stood and went to the kitchen to

grab another drink. Where was my glass? Looking left and right, and turning around to check the other side, it had vanished. Whatever. No doubt it would turn up someplace, so I opened the cupboard and took out a fresh one. Where was the whiskey? I opened door after door but didn't find it. To go out searching for it may come across as desperation, so rather than have him think worse of me, I twisted off the lid on the bottle of brandy. It wasn't high on my list of drinks to drink alone. It needed a mix. Still, I poured the honey-coloured fluid into the glass and swallowed it in two quick gulps. A violent shiver roared through me. Guess my body didn't care for brandy either.

I sat back down on my end of the couch and reached for my pizza slice. For whatever reason, I needed to keep a respectable distance from Liam, close but not too close. And I had no desire to discuss the undesirable. "So, Liam..." Time to shift the focus onto something much more pleasant. "Tell me, where did you learn to play piano?"

A smile as wide as the Grand Canyon crossed his face. "I have always loved to tickle the ivories as my father would say. My dad was this great jazz player and wrote a lot of his own music. I used to sit for hours in the parlour and listen to him and watch his fingers move as if they were independent from the rest of him. He was such a gifted musician. Sometimes, if I was good, he'd sit me on his lap and let me play a few notes. It was heavenly. After a while, I'd sneak in and play a couple of simpler songs. All by ear as I couldn't read the music."

"That's cool. I couldn't do that." My skillset from reading music was non-existent. If it weren't for *The Sound of Music,* I wouldn't even know the names of the notes on the scale.

"Sure, you could. I'll teach you if you want?" He cocked an eyebrow.

"Not me, but maybe my friend Tess. She's always on the hunt for something new and different to try."

"Nothing wrong with trying something that takes you out of your comfort zone."

"As long as it's still within your control," I said mindlessly and took a bite.

"True." He shifted in his spot and put his plate down. "Do you have a big family?"

I nearly choked on my bite of pizza. "Nope. There's just me."

"No siblings?"

Again, nope. I shook my head. No parents either which was a blessing. My parents were never in the running for parents of the year. Guess that's why I hung out at Tess's place. She had the perfect family. Suppers

121

around the table every night, a doting dad, a mom that actually cared, you know the dream.

She got perfection and I got the nightmare. A father that fleeted in and out of my life and was only in when he needed money from mother. Not that she was a peach herself. Her string of bad luck and bad decisions will haunt me for the rest of my life. Just seeing that face pop up in my mind was enough to ignite fire and rage and fear and loathing. It sounds terrible but I didn't cry when she died a couple of years back.

"Must be lonely?"

"Meh. It is what it is. I'm not complaining. I have great friends." I put my plate on the coffee table. The food wasn't as tasty as it smelled and hoped. "What about you? What's your family like?"

"Average. I have two parents and a twin sister. You met her at the airport."

"Saw her, is more like it. We didn't actually get to introductions." If Trey hadn't been there, I'm sure we would've met. She seemed like she'd be one of those that hugged everyone she met.

"Well…"

"Yeah, I know. But Trey isn't a bad guy." Not sure why I felt the need to defend the guy. I couldn't cut him from my life and yet, I wasn't exactly pulling him in close either. "He has a big heart and would give you the shirt off his back. And just as quickly bed you, if the opportunity arose." Verbal diarrhea was my nemesis. Why did that need to come out?

Liam looked down at his greasy paper plate. "It's not my business. You two have a unique relationship. It's fine by me."

"Is it though?" The words fell out before I could shove my foot into it. "I mean, I thought there was something between us. In Mexico, on the plane ride home."

"I don't know. Maybe?"

I nodded, slightly. *Maybe.*

Liam cleared his throat. "You see, the thing is, I do like you, but I can't get involved."

"Because of today?" A soft snort rolled out of me, tickling my nose.

He shook his head and an angry expression replaced the indifferent one he had a heartbeat ago. "No. Never would I use that as a reason to not go out with someone. Jesus." His hand clenched into a tight fist. "It doesn't matter what I say, you'll somehow twist it around, right?"

I recoiled in my seat and tossed my plate onto the table. "No."

He focused on the ceiling, avoiding eye contact. "I swear, they must teach women that in university. Pull you aside and teach you the finer skills about manipulation and guilt trips. Every woman has the ability to turn an ordinary statement into something negative." He ran his fingers through his thick dark hair.

"Hey, that's unfair."

"Is it?" His dark eyes pierced into my soul.

"Yes."

"You want to know why I can't get involved with you even though I really like you and enjoyed our time in Mexico together, and how I look forward to our collab time just so I can hear your laugh and smell your perfume? To watch your ideas light up your whole face and see the excitement you get in making activities fun for the students."

"Because we're colleagues?" I spit the word out like it was poison. His first day he mentioned that to Shannon.

"Jesus, woman! The reason I can't get involved with you is because of Trey. God, why can't you see that?"

Oh right. Somehow, I kept forgetting about that. Sort of. "Oh, I can see that, I just like to confirm. I'm not completely stupid. However, men dump a woman if they think in any way shape or form that she's damaged goods, so I like to remove that from the equation."

"Is that right?" He stood and towered over me.

I pushed myself out of my chair to face him. "Yeah. That's right."

"Well, guess you don't know everything." He marched to the door, and paused in a deep breath, resting his hand on the knob.

I lingered behind him, a sneer on the edge of my lips. "I know more than you'll ever understand."

"I sincerely doubt that." His shoulders fell along with his voice. "I knew a wonderful woman who committed suicide because of her apparent change in status." He turned to search out my eyes, his own having clouded over to a frighteningly haunted look. "She too thought she was damaged goods." A shuddered breath flowed out of him. "And I couldn't convince her how amazing she was. In the end, I couldn't save her."

"Oh yeah, another colleague?"

"No. My wife."

Chapter Fourteen

*H*is wife? Holy shit.

I pushed the door closed with my foot, and grabbed him by the hand, leading him into the living room where our barely eaten pizza sat.

"I'm so sorry for your loss. How long ago?"

He fell into himself as he sat on the couch. "Three years ago."

"Wow." I sat as close to him as I thought was safe. Close enough that our knees touched, but not close enough to be shoulder to shoulder, although I would've preferred that. "Tell me."

"The incident happened before I met her, in her childhood. A babysitter gone bad. As we started hanging out and getting to know each other, she'd put the brakes on us. A physical relationship was really hard for her. It was almost six months into our relationship before we did the deed." A flush coloured his cheeks. "But I didn't want to scare her, so I let her lead the way. Slowly, she revealed little details, and with each confession, I found myself falling for her and wanting to make sure something like that never happened to her, or anyone else, ever again. I became almost overprotective of her. But it was great. She was safe. We got married, and for a while, things were picture perfect. Until the day we ran into him, her old babysitter. He spoke to her, said something that she refused to tell me. After that, her whole personality changed, almost like she was sent back in time." His hands twisted so much I wondered if they were raw.

I covered them with my own and felt him relax beneath my palms. "I'm so sorry."

"The worst part was I wasn't able to protect her, no matter how much I encouraged her to share what was on her mind or to seek out professional help. Her mind was her worst enemy. It lied–" His chest rattled, and an audible breath filled the space.

"Her death wasn't your fault."

He closed his eyes. "She should've confided in me. I would've helped her, fixed her problems. Knocked the bastards lights out. I would've done anything to have made her feel better."

Slowly, I rubbed his arm, waiting for the telltale

signs of relaxing. It took a bit, but finally, his shoulders sagged, and his breath evened out. "That's very sweet of you, and I can't speak for your wife, but not all women want a man to solve their problems. Some are perfectly okay coasting through their lives without that, or think they are doing just fine without any input."

"Too bad. It's ingrained in our DNA. We're the providers, the caretakers." The look he gave me pierced into my soul. "If someone around me is hurting, I want to fix it. I need to solve the problem or make it go away. Far, far away."

I scratched my head. "Sometimes all a girl wants is comfort. We don't need someone to solve our problems or race out and tackle the source of our pain. All we need is to be held and told that together we'll get through it. One day at a time."

He wrapped an arm around me and pulled me to his chest. "Like this?"

A rock-hard lump formed, making it hard to breathe. Tears instantly filled my eyes and blurred my field of view. This wasn't about me. This was about him. His wife. Her pain.

"Together, we will get through this. One day at a time."

Damn him for throwing my words back at me. His

arms tightened around me, and I turned my head into his chest. A build-up was coming—I was standing on the edge of it—but I was fighting hard to not let it out.

"Now, I know you are troubled and bothered by what happened today, and whatever it was that happened in your past." His chest rumbled beneath my head. "I'm sorry I couldn't help you then. I'm sorry I didn't get to you in time today. I'm sorry I didn't stop him. But I promise, I won't let that happen to you ever again."

"You can't protect me. You don't even know me."

"But I want to. You just need to give me a chance."

What a change of heart. A moment ago, he wanted nothing to do with me because of Trey, and now he was begging me to give him a chance. And guys say women were confusing! Sheesh. "And Trey? How does he work into all of this?"

"You tell him what happened today. See what his reaction is."

My blood ran cold. No freaking way was I going to tell him. I had a bad day at work and that was enough for him. As big as his heart was, he didn't care about that kind of thing. If a news story came on about something like that, he always flipped it off.

"If he's an upstanding guy–"

"Which he is."

129

"Then I'll back away and the two of you can live in happiness for the rest of your days."

Thinking about the other possibility, the one where Trey doesn't find out and we split with me running into Liam's arms, had me all kinds of excited. Even though I knew Liam couldn't protect me, not that I'd want him too, there was still something about the man I yearned to learn and love. There'd been something magical about meeting him in Mexico, three thousand miles away and something fated about him coming to work at my school.

Too many things conspired to get us together. Too many things threatened to keep us apart.

"Until you give me a reason, Camille, I'm going to be here for you. At least as a friend." He kissed the top of my forehead.

I tipped my head back and through the blur in my eyes, I took him in. My lips found his, and like a dehydrated person in the desert finding an ounce of water, I drank him in.

He pulled away and looked down on me, shaking his head. "Even if I wanted to, I can't. I'm not that kind of guy. You're already spoken for."

Yeah, I was. Sort of. Geez, I really needed to work that out. Trey and I had to sit down and come to a conclusion about our relationship and what it was. If it was just sex, well, he was getting plenty of it. I wasn't the only one providing him a poking ground. But was it more? I doubted it, at least a huge part of me doubted it. A smaller part, however, wondered if the more was what kept us together. It was time to find out.

At recess the next morning, Liam poked his head into my class. "You coming?"

I knew what the emergency staff meeting was all about, and I figured it was best to avoid the whole damn thing. Saunders would completely understand, and someone would fill me in and tell me what I'd missed. "I'm good."

"It takes the pressure off you."

I cocked my eyebrow at him. "Off me? If anything, all eyes will be on me."

"Only a small handful of people know, and I'm sure those will keep the anonymity." He crossed his heart with his finger and then winked.

I pushed the pile of mixed puzzle pieces to the side of my desk and let out a long, exasperated sigh. He was so cute standing there, it made it difficult to tell him no. "Fine."

Side by side, we walked down the hall, listening to

the idle chatter of the other staff members wondering why the big emergency. Everyone shuffled into the staff room, and someone closed the door that led to the hallway where students lingered. Yep, the meeting was going to be exactly what I thought.

"Ladies and gentlemen, I'm not going to beat around the bush," Mr. Saunders said, standing at the entranceway to the staff room. "Yesterday afternoon we had an alarming situation with one of our parents against a staff member. One of our own was assaulted."

Gasps and murmurs filled the space.

I looked around at their faces pretending, like I assumed they were, trying to guess which person this happened to. No one made eye contact with me. Not even Mr. Saunders nor our custodian who was present for the meeting.

"From this moment on, we're taking extra precautionary steps to make sure this doesn't happen again."

"How did this happen to begin with? There are cameras everywhere."

Mr. Saunders acknowledged that statement. "The person entered our school on the lie that his child had forgotten something in her locker, and he was going to quickly retrieve it. This parent hadn't been suspect to do anything so malicious, so he was given access." The principal looked around the room. "I won't get into details about what happened, but I'm very glad one of our own stepped in and intervened. Things could've been a lot worse."

Questions circulated, asking who it was, who the parent was, who stopped the attack.

"For safety reasons, I won't disclose the name of the parent as it would give away the staff member, who at this time, shall remain anonymous."

"That's bullshit, Jeff." Leave it to Bernadette to speak up. I think her official title was shit disturber because she always had a reason at every staff meeting to declare why things shouldn't be done the way they were suggested. "How are we supposed to be safe from him if we don't even know who we're supposed to be wary of?"

"I understand your position, really I do. This is a very delicate matter, and we're in a bit of grey area." He gripped the back of a chair. "The parent has already been banned from stepping on the school grounds. We've consolidated with the police, and we are looking into a restraining order, but ultimately that particular staff member has to file for that. Until that point, we are working with the superintendents to do what we can, within the perimeters of the law." His gaze roved around the room, locking eyes with each person, myself included. "We have reason to believe this was a planned attack, and was very much directed at the intended party, and we are ensuring that staff member's safety."

"And you refuse to tell us the name of the parent?" Bernadette openly gawked. "So, you're really only protecting one staff member and not all of us?"

Thanks, Bernadette for that incredibly insensitive remark.

Mr. Saunders shrugged off her comment. "In moving forward, we are implementing a no teacher alone policy. Until further notice, you're not to be alone in your rooms—"

"Are you serious?" One of the grade five teachers raised her voice. "So, if I come in at 6 am to get some work done, I can't? If I need to stay after school until supper, I can't? That's complete lunacy." She slapped her hand on the table. "Why should all of us suffer?"

Mr. Saunders cleared his throat. "Georgina, I don't think you are understanding the gravity of the situation."

"Maybe you should ask us what we'd prefer? What steps we'd like implemented? How we think we should be protected and what would make sense for us to still be able to do our jobs with this nameless terrorist running around? Don't you think that we are entitled to have input into how this is handled, *moving forward?*" She air quoted him.

"Mr. Saunders, if I may?" Liam asked and stepped out from behind me, toward the center of the room. "Are you more upset that you don't know who did the attacking or how for safety reasons, a few things are going to change?" He glanced around the room. "God, I can't believe all of you. You sit here and act like he's imposing the death sentence or something. One of our co-workers was *violated*. On school property. Shouldn't you have the decency to inquire if that person is okay? And yet, not one of you did. All you cared about was how working with someone else was going to affect you."

"Liam, I think your outburst is a little uncalled for." Mr. Saunders moved closer to him and rested a hand on his shoulder.

"It's not. I'm the one that interrupted and caught the bastard attacking one of our staff. Our friend. Our *family*." He emphasised the last word. "What I saw will haunt me for a lifetime. It will most definitely haunt that person forever. And you gripe because you might need to have a buddy for safety? If this is what working here is like, I don't know that I want to be a part of this anymore."

"Liam…" I touched his arm as he stormed out of the room.

Mr. Saunders cleared his throat again, and turned

to face the staff. "Okay, moving on."

"If I can say something," I said. All eyes lasered in on me. "I think Georgina may be on to something. I don't know if the buddy system is the best idea. It's a pain in the ass. Maybe if we put our heads together, we can find another solution." I scanned the room but didn't make eye contact with anyone. Rocking on my heels, I carried on. "Perhaps, no matter what excuse they give, parents aren't allowed beyond the front hallway? If a child has forgotten something, it's their responsibility to retrieve it? Or if they are younger, then the teacher can assist them and bring the item to the front door? It's an idea. All traffic starts there. We already keep the other doors locked, so a parent isn't getting in that way."

"It's a good one." Mr. Saunders looked around the room. "I can try to be diplomatic about this." He shuffled on his feet and rested his hands on the back on a vacant chair. "Why don't you all submit your ideas to me, and we can discuss this at length? But for now, please be vigilant. If anything seems off, bring it to my attention."

"Jeff?" A meek voice from the corner of the room called out. "Is she okay?"

Mr. Saunders scanned the room and inhaled. "In outward appearances, it would seem so. No one can see the battle she's dealing with on the inside, so be nice to your co-workers. Give a little more love to each other, be kind and helpful. You all mean a great deal to me and I'd hate to have another incident to happen."

"And there's absolutely no way you'll tell us who the parent is?" Bernadette asked again. She elbowed her assistant and mumbled something to her. I couldn't make out the phrasing.

"As I've stated before, that is up to the victim. They will need to file a restraining order, and that would ensure that the parent stays off the school grounds, and if it was broken, the police would be here in record time." He quickly locked eyes with me before moving on. "However, until our staff member gets that order, I'm afraid I'm not at liberty to discuss."

A swallow of building bitterness lodged in my throat. It was on me to vocalise his name. If I said his name, it would expose that I was his intended target. It would also make everyone a little more at ease in knowing who they should be watching out for, and in a way, maybe they'd watch out for me. I took a deep breath and clasped my hands together. "It was Dalton Murdoch."

Chapter Fifteen

L istening to staff talk about how nice a man Dalton was when they thought I couldn't hear, made me nauseous. Without a word or any further explanations, I left and marched to my wing of the school. Liam's door was open, and I poked my head inside.

"You okay?"

He looked up and gave his eyes a rub. In the span of a few minutes, he seemed like he's aged a few years. "I should be asking you that."

I pursed my lips together and sat on one of the tables. "It is what it is. I told them it was Dalton."

He rose from his desk and headed over to me. "You didn't have to. Jeff would've made sure that stayed under wraps."

"I know." My head drooped and my shoulders sagged. "It, oddly enough, felt good to say his name. Like it took away some of his power or something."

Liam tipped my chin with a hook of his finger. "I'm proud of you. That's a hard thing to admit."

"No. The hard part was listening to the staff. Some believed that he was a nice man."

"Nice men don't hurt women. Ever. There's no excuse." He shook his head.

"Well, for the next few lunches I'll eat in my room, no-teacher-alone-policy be damned. I don't need to hear about Murdoch's accolades, not do I want to hear their soft voices or see their pitiful looks. I'm perfectly fine without any of that."

"It won't be as bad as you think."

I nodded. "Sure."

This wasn't the first time. Years ago, before I met Tess, it had happened. I was eight, he was ten. The jerk thought it was funny to pin me against the stairs on the portable and grope and kiss me in front of his friends, very much like Dalton Murdoch did. The students all cheered despite me trying to push Easton Sawyer away. After that, Easton became a hero and I was a branded slut and floozy. At eight! I didn't even know what those words meant but I quickly learned. Until Tess arrived at school, friendships were abandoned, girls looked at me with hatred in their eyes. But not the boys. Thanks to Easton, I'd captured all their attention and not in a good way.

It took years of honing and perfecting it, but I made it work for me rather than against me and almost in a revenge-like way, I got the boys to do whatever I asked. In return, they got a little favour. But I had the control. The upper hand. Back then. Somehow, I lost it yesterday.

The bell rang, recess was over, as was my time with Liam.

Shaking away the memory, I pulled my hair over my shoulder. "Anyways, I just wanted to say thanks. For yesterday, for last night, for today."

"Anytime."

I moved toward the door and paused as he called out my name.

"Camille..."

A sharp inhale of air filled my lungs.

"You're worth it, you know."

It was a lie, and I knew it. Without a look back, I met with my students.

After school pickup was a breeze. My five standard late students hung out with Mr. Donaldson and me. As each arrived, Liam was kind enough to stress to the parents how important it was to be punctual as it was important to the child that they were not always last. He kept it professional and light, yet there was an undercurrent tone that suggested he was completely serious.

I held my breath as Edalyn, the nanny, rounded the corner. She slowly staggered towards me but kept a distance. "Off you go, Lily."

It took a little bit of convincing, but the little girl finally made her way over to her caregiver and they joined Lily's older sister. Edalyn kept turning to look at me. The most serious expression on her face, but no words escaped her mouth.

I wondered if she knew. I also wondered if she'd been a recipient to her employer's conduct.

Liam escorted me to class and hung out near the door while I packed my things.

"Would you like to join me for supper tonight?" he asked, crossing one leg over the other as he struck a model-like pose and leaned casually against the door jam.

"I really would like to, but I think I should be alone tonight."

"Are you sure that's the best idea?"

I didn't but rolled with it. Being alone in the physical sense was new territory. Usually, I'm alone emotionally and mentally. "Yeah, I think it's for the best."

"Is your boyfriend expected over?" There was no

hostility in his comment, just concern.

"No. He's supposed to be working the one to nine tonight." That was his typical Tuesday schedule and sometimes he popped by afterwards for a little nightcap. We'd see if it happened tonight.

I sent a few documents to the office printer to grab before I let the secretary know I was leaving. Closing out of everything, I grabbed my bag and made my way to Liam.

"I'll walk you to the door."

"It's not necessary."

"It's Saunder's rule, remember?"

How could I forget? The incident only happened yesterday and yet, it felt like moments ago and a lifetime ago. Emotions were weird that way.

Liam and I practically tiptoed through the hallway to the front office. It never failed to amaze me just how quickly a school loses its sound at the end of the day. When the students were around, there was a hum and murmur of children talking and playing in their rooms, of walking in the hallways trying their best to be quiet, and of course, the raucous sounds of yelling and laughter echoing out of the gym.

With the students dismissed, the halls became a ghost town, devoid of all but the eeriest of noises, like a wind blowing through a crack in a window. I shuddered at the feeling.

I scooped a random mitt left on the ground, a stray sock, and a notebook, depositing them into the lost and found.

Printouts in my hand, I waved to the secretary and without a word headed out the main door, Liam close at my feet.

"I've got this." My shoulders back and my head held high, my confidence a weak mask for the puddle of mush inside. As much as I claimed I was all good on my own, I was thankful for the company. Even if he didn't say much and the only sounds were our shoes rubbing against the concrete sidewalks.

My car was right where I parked it yesterday, and since Liam took me home after the Murdoch incident, he made sure to pick me up. Although it had been thirty-three hours since the start of the workweek, it had felt like a small lifetime. I unlocked my door with a sudden desire to get home, soak in a bath and go to bed.

Liam hung on the door as I slipped into the driver's seat. "If you need anything, you call me, okay?"

"Will do. Same for you." It wasn't hard to miss how bothered by the incident he was. He'd become overprotective in a way, and not just with me. I'd noticed it with all the female staff, although Shannon was hoping for a little more personal protection.

He cocked his eyebrow. "I'm fine." He closed my car door and lingered beside the stall, giving me a quick wave as I pulled away. Even in the rear-view mirror, he remained.

I drove to my apartment, after a quick stop at the liquor store. The missing bottle of whiskey never reappeared and needed replacing. At home, with the door locked and chained, I poured myself a tall glass of the amber-coloured fluid and downed half of it, relishing the burn from the back of my throat into the pit of my stomach.

Glass in hand, I teetered a few steps down the hall and started running a bath. While the water lapped against the bottom and slowly inched up the sides, I poured in some freesia scented bath salts and oils. My skin was showing signs of neglect and was in desperate need of rejuvenating. Even my hair was limp and my skin sallow. The past few days had not only trampled across my memories, drudging up the bad feelings, but they'd worn their footprints across my face. I was only twenty-five, but I looked like I was pushing forty. Unacceptable.

Stripping out of my clothes, I prepped myself for a mini spa day, complete with a hair and facial mask. It was heavenly slipping under the hot, silky water and stretching out. Music played from my phone, a soothing collection of wind instruments and birds chirping and crocking frogs. I downed the rest of my whiskey and submerged myself up to my shoulders, closing my eyes and focusing on the subtle beats of music and trying to guess how many different birds there were.

A jolt and a shudder, I splashed my arms through the tepid water. *Holy shit!* I'd fallen asleep in the tub and had been in there for three hours. Peeling the mask from my face, along with the first layer of skin, I attempted to stand up. My water-logged body weighed two hundred pounds, and it was like moving through mud. Every movement was slow and deliberate. I unwound the towel wrapped around my head and stared at the gluey mess piled there.

My bath had been too relaxing, and now I needed a shower to clean myself up. Great.

The water ran out of the showerhead cold enough to make me gasp but slowly it warmed up. I stood under it, allowing the gentle pulse to massage my head and rinse away the conditioner that had dried to a sticky paste. I tipped my head and had the water pulse against the raw skin on my face while I gently massaged it clean. Running my hands over my chest, I froze and righted my head.

Yesterday I'd been on a mission to scrub myself

clean and uncomfortable sensations arose when I touched myself. I blamed the fact that Liam was in the living room waiting on me as the reason for not pushing the issue.

But this was new. My body reacted violently to my own touch. A surge of adrenaline pounded through my body.

"It's me," I told myself out loud. "It's only me." I inhaled a few quick breaths and pulled open the shower curtain to stare at my reflection. "See?" As if that helped. But it did.

I watched as my hands ran along the swell of my boobs and under them, gently cupping them. An involuntary moan escaped me. It wasn't a good sound. Curiously, my focus jumped to my face to watch my reaction while the heartbeat in my ears drowned out any sound.

"You're safe." My eyes focused on my reflected fingertips while they gently rubbed and caressed my nipples, turning them into hard little peaks beneath the touch. "Yes. All good. Totally safe. I won't hurt you."

Hand on my boob, I allowed my other hand to navigate south. Slowly. Gently. With caution. Over the defined core muscles, counting out the ribs my fingers ran over. Across the cute little belly button I'd always wanted to pierce but never had the courage to. My pulse at an epic speed, just shy of its max beat, but as I watched my hand in the mirror, I knew I was in control.

My chest tightened, and a weird tingling sensation spread out to my fingertips.

Gliding my wet hand lower, I stopped just above my pubic area, the soft down reminding me I was due for another waxing appointment. My other hand dropped from my boob and hung out at my hip.

I challenged myself as I talked to my reflection. "You've got this. You are in control."

My hand inched lower. I nodded. My breathing became sharp as my hand pushed against the taut skin and cupped my lower luscious lips. I checked myself out. I was all alone. I was safe. I was in charge.

My finger wiggled itself against the most intimate part of me and fired up a round of interesting and happy sensations. Instinctively, I lifted my leg and gave into the wandering touches and flicks and feelings. A groan rolled out of me as I found and massaged my happy spot.

Freeing the showerhead from its holding, I aimed it perfectly, and surrendered to the building sensations that threatened to rip me apart. I held it steady and gasped, the intensity sending out ripples of excitement to the tips of my curled toes and my tensed fingertips. My breathing shallowed and I was getting lightheaded, but I was so close to release I just needed to hold on for a few more seconds.

The seconds passed, the buildup plateaued and racing disappointment that it'll never happen threatened on the sidelines. I closed my eyes and imagined Liam, with his hot, tanned body pressed against me, arms wrapped around me as he sent me off to the sky. It was his hot mouth between my legs, not a jet of water. It took every ounce of imagination to make it work, and after a small lifetime, the surge of a sub-par orgasm rippled through me. The showerhead held tightly in my hands sprayed the bathroom as I shuddered, sending pulses of water over the mirror and vanity.

But I did it. I regained control of my body. It was mine to explore freely, and in my imagination, I had surrendered it to only one other. Liam. However, that realisation came with a heaping side of guilt; guess it was time to end things with Trey.

Turning the water off, another wave of emotion washed over me. Unable to stand from the mounting guilt and frustration, I sat on the end of the tub and succumbed to the tears and hurt and anger and despair over everything that had gone on in the last few days. My eyes watered and my breathing caught, but after a few minutes of soul-crushing sobbing and hysterics, I actually felt lighter.

Chapter Sixteen

At nine-thirty that evening, I lightly rapped my knuckles against Trey's door. He didn't answer, which was odd. By this point, he should've been home. I knocked again. No answer.

I staggered back toward the stairwell, my feet dragging with each step. My hand was on the door when it was yanked free from my weak grip. "Oh, pardon me," I said and stepped aside, staring at the two sets of feet.

"Cammy?"

Oh great, it was Trey. And judging from the nice set of heels standing beside him, a woman. "Hey." I chanced a look at him.

He stepped toward me. "You look… rough."

"Thanks," I breathed out.

He waved a hand in front of his nose. "And you smell rough too."

It was a victory drink. A toast to my regaining control. However, Trey didn't need to know that. His comment was said to with the effect of making himself look big around the voluptuous lady waiting to sink his claws into him. "Again, thanks."

The girl beside him purred. "Trey."

"Just a second. This is one of my friends."

Ah, friends. Even in my slightly inebriated state, I felt the full weight of those words. To the outside world, we were just friends. Alone, or when I was around a cool guy, he was my boyfriend. A sigh fell out of me as I leaned against the wall. My legs were turning into jelly, making it very difficult to stand properly.

Trey leaned closer to me. "How much have you been drinking?"

"Just a little." I squished my thumb and finger together at eye level to check.

Trey shook his head of golden frizz. I loved running my fingers through the thick of it but only after he showered. Most of the time when he'd come home from work, his hair would be greasy and grungy from working over the deep fryers. "Another bad day?" he asked as the girl tugged on his arm.

"Actually, today was a good day." No douchebag, my students co-operated, and Liam was ultra sweet.

"Umm, I see."

My reason for wandering the hall though in my fleecy bathrobe with a cute two-piece pajama set on... "I wanted to talk to you."

"Is it urgent? Can it wait?" He subtly tipped his head to the brunette beside him.

"I guess." Now that I've seen him bringing home a tramp in person, I wanted to end things even faster. But waiting wouldn't hurt me. Being that I should've dumped him a long time ago, what's another twenty-four hours? I staggered to the stairwell. "I'll be home tomorrow after five. Come over when you finish work." The door was heavy as I pushed it open, and I barely managed to make it through before it bumped me on the ass.

The first step was a doozy and I slipped, banging my head against the wall.

A second later, Trey stood at the doorway, a look of amusement and genuine concern mixed across his features. "I'll walk you up to your apartment."

"Why? I'll be fine. Go back to your little honey." I rubbed the side of my head that had connected with the wall.

"I heard that," she called out from down the hall.

Whatever, lady. You're truly the least of my worries. Right now, my biggest concern was how I was going to crawl up a flight of stairs without looking like a drunk person. It would be a test of endurance and one for the record books.

"I'll be right back, Charla." Trey hoisted me onto my feet. "Easy does it."

I clutched at his shoulders and gasped. No way was I going to fall down the stairs.

Trey turned his head away from me. "How much did you drink? You smell like a brewery."

"Sometimes it's easier to deal with life when it doesn't sting as much." I leaned against Trey's strong body as he slowly climbed the flight of stairs. Each step was a huge effort and by the time we reached my floor, I was exhausted and ready for bed, and I'd already taken a three-hour nap in the tub.

"There are better ways, you know?"

"Hmph. I doubt that." The floor suddenly started spinning and I grabbed the hand railing as Trey opened the door. It hadn't been that much to drink. Just enough to take the edge off. I've easily had more than that before, so why was it affecting me so strongly? Had I bought a tainted bottle that was somehow laced with another substance. "Wow."

"Wow, what?"

"I think someone poisoned my booze."

152

Trey had to audacity to laugh. "I doubt that."

"Then why can't I walk?" Indeed, it was like I had to convince myself to move each foot forward. They weren't doing it without step-by-step instruction and my brain was too tired to think it through anymore.

"Because you had too much to drink." He rolled his eyes. Yeah, that wasn't helpful.

"I didn't, though." I'd drank just enough to forget the reasoning behind the need to drink for.

My apartment was the first door past the stairway, and we arrived. I unhooked my lanyard from around my neck and unlocked my apartment. Even going down a level to Trey's place, I never failed to lock it. Too many creeps out there.

"In you go." Trey assisted me in and closed the door. He stopped at the kitchen and held the fresh bottle of whiskey. "Is this new?"

"Yep. Bought it today." It was even on sale, lucky me.

"It's half gone, Cam." His shortening my name was the equivalent to a parent middle-naming you. He waved the bottle in my face. The liquid sloshed from side to side.

However, I was a grown-ass adult and I rolled my eyes. "You're good."

"This is a 750ml bottle."

"I'm still not getting what the problem is? I've had two glasses since four o'clock." Like seriously, it's been five and a half hours. That really isn't that much alcohol to consume over that time frame.

"Glasses or shots?"

Giving him a slow, satisfyingly smug look, I lifted the 8oz glass. I'd never actually owned shot glasses.

Shaking his head, he tucked the bottle into the pocket of his jacket.

"That's mine." I went to snatch it back, but he jumped away. Damn, he was quick.

"Have you eaten since you got home?"

That was a really good question. Had I? Hmm. I retraced my steps since coming home. A lightbulb came on. "Nope." Hadn't had a bite at all. In fact, I even skipped lunch. Which explained why I was feeling so good. It wasn't poison added to my whiskey, it's that I'd had nothing to help absorb the alcohol.

"You need to eat."

"I need a lot of things right now. Food isn't high on my list." I staggered backwards and my calves hit the edge of the couch. Toppling over, I landed on my side on the cushions. "Make the room stop spinning."

Trey hunched in front of me. "I almost want you to suffer through this drunken escapade." He wiped away the tendrils of hair hanging in my eyes. "But I think you're already suffering enough in here." A dull tap bounced on my forehead. "I'll send Charla home, and I'll be right back with food." He stood and wiggled my key. "I'll lock up."

"Don't go," I said in a whimper.

Trey lowered himself so we were eye level again. "I can't just leave her down there."

Tears pooled in my eyes and ran over the bridge of my nose, falling onto the cushion. "I love you." It came out in a whisper, but it was loud and clear in my head.

He sighed and rubbed my shoulder. "I'll be back in a bit. Give me five minutes."

I wiped my eyes. "It's okay. Stay with your lady friend and I'll see you tomorrow. I'll be fine." The couch was oddly comfortable, and although the room was tipping, it was easier to handle than trying to navigate the hall to my room. "I'm just going to go to sleep and put this day behind me. I'll be fine. Honestly."

He lifted himself and sat on the coffee table. "What am I going to do with you?" It was whispered, but still loud enough to hear. Pulling the cuff of his sweatshirt to his fingers, he mopped my pool of tears. "Will you tell me what's been bugging you lately?"

"There's no point."

An exasperated sigh rolled out of him. "Cammy."

It wasn't that I didn't trust Trey, because I did. He'd never hurt me, and I knew that. But I couldn't trust myself to tell him. Perhaps it was self-preservation and the need to keep up the act that I was strong enough to handle everything life threw at me, but he was the type of person that hearing something like that would lash out and rage. Not on me, but on a very specific target. As wonderful as it would be to have Murdoch's lights punched out, I didn't want Trey going to jail, because that's exactly how my luck ran.

I looked up at Trey from my now comfy, yet still tipping from side to side position on the couch. "Honestly, go back to your girl before she leaves. I'll talk to you tomorrow."

"Do I need to get you anything?"

"Just my phone." I closed my eyes. It didn't help to stop the spinning.

"Where's that?"

Hell if I knew. "Kitchen?"

He checked and flashed it in my direction before setting it on the coffee table. "I'll check on you later?"

"I hope I'll be sleeping." My eyelids were exceptionally heavy.

He planted a kiss on my forehead. "I'll see you for dinner tomorrow? We can discuss whatever it was you wanted to talk about tonight."

"Okay."

Trey covered me with the throw blanket. "Tomorrow."

I closed my eyes and listened as he shuffled to the door, which clicked as he shut it. The deadbolt slid into its holding and a weird sound came from underneath. I peered through tiny slits in my tired eyes and spotted the lanyard on the floor. That's what he pushed under. "Good night, Liam."

Chapter Seventeen

I dashed into my classroom just as the bell rang and tossed my bag toward my desk. The contents spilled across the floor, a litter of unsorted fabric swatches and a bin of rice and plastic farm animals reminded me of the work I didn't accomplish last night. "Damn it." Oh well, they'd need to stay there for now. My students were expecting me at their door.

Walking with purpose, I rounded the corner and spotted Liam, dressed in a pair of black jeans and a button-up. It said casually dressed, but really, on him, it was a smart combination. He looked amazingly sexy and yet, ready to play with the kids. They were so lucky to have all the fun.

"Morning," I said, strutting over to him, my waves nice and bouncy thanks to the over-conditioning treatment they were awarded.

He gave me a solid once over and my ego inflated just a touch at the way his eyes lingered over my face. "Good morning." His strong hand reached out and pushed the door open, and the children raced inside, pushing and shoving against the others. He dropped his hand to their level. "Easy does it." As the children walked by, he met my gaze. "Did you have a nice evening?"

"I got lots of sleep."

His dark eyes studied mine. "Good. A recharge is always important."

"Yeah. I didn't realise I needed quite so much."

"It happens. Self-care is very important." A small child, Darian I thought, clung to his leg in a quick hug.

Oh, I got some self-care last night. Sex was an important part of who I was, and I'll be damned if I was going to let some asshole take that away from me. And when, or if, Trey and I hooked up again, I wanted to make sure I'd be able to handle it. I think I'm good. Besides, I trusted Trey. But it wasn't him I wanted as much. I stared at Liam.

His head was tipped to the side and his hands were folded in front of him.

"I'm sorry?" It was like he'd said something, and I missed out on it.

"I asked what you did last night."

159

I shook my head. "Sorry. Lost in thought. Anyways, I gave myself a facial and hair treatment. It was time." And drank myself into a stupor too.

He stepped closer to me, so close that students could not pass between us. "Personally, I think you're stunning."

I held my breath, unbelieving. This morning I looked pale and deeply hungover. However, it was a sweet thing to say.

He put a little space between us just as I was reaching down to touch his hand. "Do you have lunch plans?"

"Actually, yeah. I was going to make up for all the time I lost last night and attempt to catch up."

"May I join you?" The last of our students walked in and we closed the door, double-checking that it was latched.

My mouth suddenly went dry and I nodded an affirmative to his invitation, walking in step with him.

The grade one teacher, an elderly lady two years away from retiring, gave me a soft smile. It used to be a warm and genuine one, but it was like she was holding back. In fact, she stepped out of the way as I approached.

"Good morning," I said.

"Morning." She disappeared into her class.

I sighed. "You'd think I'm diseased or something." It was getting tiresome being avoided. I wasn't going to pass on my bad luck just by talking to them, I wished they understood that.

"They're just being cautious."

"By avoiding..." I bit my tongue. "You know, rather than avoid me, maybe they could..." What? What was it I wanted from them? Mainly to not be treated any differently, but obviously, that wasn't going to happen. I still wanted the interaction, the connection, the fun we used to have. Now it felt like me vs the world and that wasn't the fun I desired. I stopped at my door. "See you at recess?"

"Supervision."

"Lunch it is." I winked and danced into my class.

Lunch couldn't come fast enough. The warm weather had fired up the wiggle bugs in my herd, and they were antsy. We needed to interrupt our regular centers with a dance mix every thirty minutes. At least the morning flew by and I dismissed my morning group with ease.

Returning from dismissal, I switched from the kids' dance music over to a more soothing classical mix with the sound of rolling waves in the background. So much nicer. Even a little romantic.

Liam strode in all sexy and confident. "Lunchtime."

I lowered the volume on the smartboard. "Have a seat." I pointed to a round table I'd just washed in Lysol wipes.

"You know, I heard there was a garden here."

"There is." It was all fenced in and only accessible from inside of the school. Personally, I'd never been in it. It was used with the upper elementary kids and one of their science units.

"Is there a bench there? It's a beautiful day and I figured it would be nice to eat outside."

"I honestly don't know."

"Let's check it out. Be adventurous." He winked and I wanted to fall into a puddled mess. How did he manage to charm me so? Especially since he was keeping a distance because of Trey.

I rooted through my bag and grabbed my meager lunch. In my haste this morning, I'd tossed in an orange and a protein bar. Truly though, it was all the calories I needed. Lunch in hand, I walked over to him. "I'll lead the way."

"You'd better."

He was close enough that I could've linked my

hand through his, but I held back. He wasn't ready for that, even if I was. Trey was a moot point. Things between us would be ending tonight.

I pushed open the door to the garden and was instantly taken into another world. Giant planters with a variety of different coloured leaves sat around. I touched the leaves amazed that they were already growing. It was only April, and although it was warm, parts of the city still had snow. The leaves were slippery and plastic. Totally fake. Making my way over to the ivy vines wrapped themselves through the chain-link fence, I felt them, discovering that they were not real. Too bad, although it gave the space a decent amount of privacy. The area itself was put on the far side of the school away from the field and playground. The loud squeals and laughs were audible, but that was about it. I assumed the two cedar trees were part of the reason. The bottoms were still covered, so I guessed that they were a recent addition.

Liam pointed to the bench bathed in the full sun and I sat, turning my face toward the bright light. "I've missed this."

Liam sat beside me. "If I close my eyes, I can make believe I'm in Mexico."

"No beach though."

"No."

The beach was nice. I enjoyed it, not near as much as Tess did. The rolling waves were a part of her DNA I was sure. I preferred sunbathing and a quick dip in the pool.

"I wished the trip was longer." Liam's voice broke through my reveries.

I peeled open my eyes. "I wished that too. Or that I'd gotten to know you earlier in the trip." Like Tess had with Jon. Day one she met him, whereas, with Liam, it had been day five.

"We'll always have Mexico." There was a hint of sadness in the last word.

"I'm sorry I never said anything about Trey."

He turned to me. "Actually, I'm glad you didn't."

"What?"

"If you had, I wouldn't have hung around with you and ended my vacation on a high note. I would've been hanging out with my buddies and listening to the endless ways they droned on and on about the resort."

"They didn't like it?" What was not to like? Free drinks, free food, endless hot guys parading around, rooms to die for in their size and comfort.

"The crowd wasn't young enough. Apparently. They did go to the sister resort a few times and hooked up."

"What about you? Did you hook up?" Judging from the tense neck muscles and the hunched shoulders, I'd say no. I knew he hadn't with me, but we just didn't have enough time to get to know each other first.

"Not what I was there for."

I nodded. "Same. I came because Tess needed to get away. It was a total last-minute whim, but I'm glad I went."

"Because?" A smile edged out.

"Two reasons really." I leaned against the brick wall, enjoying the natural warmth of the sun. "I got to watch my best friend fall in love. It was so amazing to see her crawl out of her shell with Jon and do all the things she'd always dreamed of doing. She put aside her insecurities and just did it. And in the process of doing that, she found herself. The person I always knew she was, but she hadn't yet realised for herself. It was something else. And she's so happy. Not just because she has a new man, but because she's just all lit up inside. She changed. For the better."

Liam leaned his head against the brick wall. "That's something."

I couldn't help but smile. "It really is. Jon lives in Maine though, so they're struggling a little with making a long-distance relationship work, but I have a feeling in here…" I placed my hand over my heart and gasped at the sensation of touching my boob. It took my breath away for a heartbeat, but only for a moment. "I believe that it'll work out perfectly. It's true love. It has to."

"You believe that?"

I softly snorted. I wasn't a romantic by any stretch but yeah, a part of me trusted that there was the perfect person for everyone out there. "I have to."

"Why?"

I stared into Liam's eyes, all dark and curious. "Because the fairy tales can't be wrong."

"And if you were a fairy tale, which one would you be?"

"That's personal." But without skipping a beat, I knew who I most identified with. It wasn't hard for me to see I wasn't like Ariel, or Belle, or Mulan, or Pocahontas.

"I don't see that."

"Of course, you don't. You're a guy. But us girls. For the most part, we want the whole story. For our own prince charming to rescue us, sort of, and give us a life…" I tugged down my skirt and stared at my feet as I made little circles with them. In my head, the idea sounded better, romantic even, but as the words slipped out it sounded childish. "You're right, it's stupid. And not feminist at all." If any other female heard me say that, I'd probably be raked over the coals. It's not like I needed or wanted to be rescued, because I hardly thought of myself as a damsel in distress. I was more manly than most of the girls I knew. I could change a tire on my car and knew enough basic plumbing and electrical to fix a minor problem. I didn't need a man in my life for that. However, I wanted a prince who would sweep me off my feet and treat me like a princess and respect me.

"It's not stupid, and I'm deeply curious where you're going with this."

I had his undivided attention and suddenly, I became uncomfortable. My hands curled around the bench seat and I put my weight into it. I broke away from his stare. "Never mind."

He opened his lunch bag and unwrapped a sandwich. "What was the other reason?"

"Huh?"

"You said you had two reasons you were glad you went to Mexico, the first being your friend Tess."

Heat bloomed across my cheeks the way I imagined the flowers budded out here in the sun—fast. "Well, you're the other reason."

"I'm flattered."

I playfully pushed him. "You knew that."

"I'd hoped, but no, I didn't know."

Looking around, I was checking for security cameras, but I didn't see any. They'd be hard to miss. Thankful we weren't being watched, I linked my hand through his. He didn't protest as I predicted.

"I'm breaking up with Trey tonight." The words fell out before I could stop them. "I want there to be something more between you and me."

"I don't want to be the reason you break up."

Oh my gawd, I was so confused, and I was sure that jumped on to my face.

"Don't mistake my words. I want to be with you and see where things go with us, but I don't want you to end it with him because of me. I want you to end it because it's the right thing to do. I'm not going to pry into how your relationship works, because he seems like a nice guy, a genuine guy. One I can probably be friends with."

"That would be weird."

"Maybe. But my point is, if your relationship was strong and lovey-dovey, you and I wouldn't have happened. There's a weak link in your chain, and you exploited it."

"I don't think I *exploited* it per se, but maybe I explored with not being with him."

"I don't want to be the greener grass on the other side."

I released his hand. "I'll have you know that trip to Mexico was the first time I've ever cheated on anyone. I'm not a habitual cheater or anything. For all intents and purposes, it was a revenge cheat."

"Lower your voice," Liam said, putting his hand level in the air and lowering it.

I hadn't been aware that I was getting so loud, but Liam had to know the truth. I wasn't a cheater; I'd just been lax on letting go of Trey before I did anything about it. A gush of air sailed over my lips. "Trey's been cheating on me for a long time. What I did in Mexico before I met you was revenge."

"Awesome." He pushed away from me.

"Hey," I said, my volume increasing again. "Where do you get off?"

"It's cool, you don't get it. That's fine. Maybe it was a bad idea."

"Like what? Us?" *Please don't say yes.*

"I want you to figure that out. You need to know what you want from a relationship before you go pursuing another. And once you know that, come find me and we'll take it from there."

I stood. "I don't understand you, Liam Donaldson. You say you want to be with me, and when I tell you I'm dumping the guy I'm with to be with you, you get all...

169

female on me." It wasn't the right word, but he was so wishy-washy in his feelings it was hard to get a grasp on exactly what I was supposed to be wanting from him.

"I'm trying to be nice." He rose and faced me. "You need to understand, if you go straight from him to me, I'm going to worry the whole time that you're just looking for something better to come along. You need to be with Trey, or not be with him, for reasons that have zero to do with me and everything to do with you. Do you get that? I won't be your runner up prize."

Ouch. I slumped onto the bench as he opened the door and disappeared into the school. Liam wasn't a participation prize and he needed to know that. But how could I prove that to him?

Chapter Eighteen

Maybe it was my mood, the whole abrupt ending to a lunch that had been going nicely. I'd felt like we were connecting on a different level, almost like we were in Mexico. Back then, it had only been us. Lunch had been the same way. Just us. And then he had to say what he said. How was I supposed to respond to that?

I stormed to my room and shut the door. Misery hung over me like a dark cloud. It was impossible to keep my sour mood from tainting the start of the afternoon class, and I reminded myself several times that the students were not to blame.

Sighing, I sat at the numeracy station and worked with a couple of children.

"Miss Evans?" Lily's voice whined as she walked over to me. "I don't feel well."

"Where?"

"My tummy."

"Okay, time to go to the office." Sick kids were a no-go in my room. If they were sick, they were going home. I didn't need to catch it, and if the other kids in the class got it, it always took a few more out with it. "Mrs. Barrie?" I called my assistant over.

"Yes."

"Lily's not feeling well. Can you take her to the office and have them call home?" There was no way in hell I was making that call.

"Sure thing."

"I want you." Lily clung onto my bicep and rested her head on my shoulder.

"I can't." *Because your dad is fucking creepy.* "I need to stay here with your friends. But Mrs. Barrie will take good care of you." I didn't want to be mean to Lily after all that went down, but at the same time, I needed to keep my distance. I pushed her off me and over to my assistant.

"Come on, let's get your bag."

Lily stopped at the garbage can and threw up.

Ugh. "Take that with you," I instructed Mrs. Barrie. No sense in having that smell lingering in the class. With Lily gone, I retrieved the disinfecting wipes and cleaned the spots where Lily had hung out, just to be on

172

the safe side. She'd only been in class for thirty minutes, but germs spread like wildfire.

I paced around the room and helped out other students, always glancing at the door. Not sure why, but I had an impending sense of doom. A few minutes later, Mrs. Barrie came back.

"That was quick." I hadn't expected pick up to be so fast.

"The office got a hold of someone and they're on their way."

The nanny, I assume. Wonder what she did all day while the kids were in school. Not that it was any of my business. I was just glad that Lily was going home to rest and feel better. I went about my work and read them a story before gym time.

Liam's class joined ours as usual, but today was different as he kept to one side of the gym. Our Vice Principal, an energetic triathlete, was leading our large group in a fun game of Lighthouse and Ships. I gave her the signal I'd be back in three minutes since I desperately needed to use the bathroom.

She gave me the thumbs up and I gave a fleeting look to Liam before I snuck out the side door. I moved lightning fast down the hall to the staff room where the appropriately sized toilets awaited. With a little luck, I made it in time and breathed out a sigh of relief.

Finishing up, I walked through the staff room, passed Saunder's closed office door toward the secretary's desk.

She glanced up from her work as I approached.

"I just wanted to check that Lily got picked up…" It was almost 2 pm. I'd sent her down over an hour ago. The secretary's gaze darted out the hallway and my heart sunk. "She's still here?" Sick children recovered better at home than they did on a couch at school. I was just about to head out into the hallway to check when the secretary rose.

"Don't go out there." Her words a warning sending a chill down my back.

I started inching toward Saunder's office, begging my feet to move faster.

Like a bolt of lightning, he was suddenly at the entrance to the office. His twisted smile smacked me in the face. "Good afternoon, Miss Evans." The very words were laced with such a sweetness it turned my stomach.

He's not supposed to be here. The ban said so. My feet froze to the ground and my mouth dried out. I couldn't choke out a word if my life depended on it. Several came to mind, but nothing came out.

The secretary, a tiny little thing no taller than five

feet, pounced out from behind her desk and stood between us. "You can take Lily home now." Jane tried to break up the horrifying stare he sent in my direction by waving her hands around. "I'll sign her out. Bye-bye."

"I thought I'd have a little word with Miss Evans since she's right here." The smile he pasted onto his thick, bearded face was revolting. It wasn't sincere and reeked with bad vibes.

"Don't move another inch toward me." Finally, words flowed out. My hands had curled into tight little fists and the adrenaline racing through me was enough to propel me forward into him, swinging and punching with all my might.

Murdoch didn't move but his eyes narrowed like he was readying to send murderous daggers towards me.

"It's time for you to leave. Take your daughter home." My words were tight and clipped and rude in tone, but I didn't give a damn. "Is there a code we can call out?" If he advanced, I was a goner. I'd never be able to take him. But somewhere in this building Saunders was around, and he'd back me up. I lifted the receiver to the phone on the desk beside me. "Where's Saunders?"

She continued to wave her arms. "Colton."

That was code for a meeting with the other principals, conducted off-site at Colton Academy.

Hopefully, the asshole glaring at me figured it was another teacher's room in the school. I fought to keep my shoulders squared and my wits about me. Calling the cops was high on my list but it'd take them a bit to get here since I had no restraining order against Murdoch and I'd never pressed charges. It would likely be pushed down on their priority list, especially since Murdoch was doing nothing more than standing there, undressing me with his dirty eyes.

"Not calling?"

A shudder built and I bit my tongue, lifting the phone receiver higher in threat. "It's time for you to go home." Where the hell was Wentworth?

Murdoch didn't move.

"Yes, Lily needs you," the secretary added, pointing to the child I couldn't see from my vantage point but did happen to see on the monitor behind Jane's desk

Yes, please think of your daughter.

My grip tightened on the phone. Fuck it. I'd put out a general call that would ring into everyone's classes.

He failed to make a move toward Lily and instead advanced on Jane.

I punched in the code to address the entire school. "Wentworth to the office immediately." Despite my brevity, my voice cracked as my finger slipped over the end button.

In one swift move, Murdoch picked Jane up and moved her off to the side like she was a toy, and he stepped alarming quick in my direction. Unfortunately, I was trapped since the u-shaped desk had only one opening and Murdoch was blocking it.

"I just want to talk." It was an attempt at being soothing but it did nothing to calm me down.

Jane disappeared into the hallway.

My heart plummeted into my stomach. *Don't leave me alone.* But I could only watch her from the corner of my eye, Murdoch was stalking me like prey to a kill.

"You'd better stop right there."

"Or what?" A devilish grin spread over his face. "I like it when a gal's feisty."

The thought rippled through me and I prayed my legs wouldn't collapse out from under me.

Jane's tiny voice was loud. "Hurry. Quick."

Wentworth pounded into the office, with Liam quick on his heels. "Step away from her." It sounded like a growl and if my hairs weren't already on edge, that would've done it.

Murdoch didn't even give them the time of day. Instead, he directed his comment to me. "I only want to be your friend."

The door to the office closed, leaving only

Wentworth, Liam, Murdoch and I sharing the same air. My eyes quickly darted to the camera above Murdoch's head. This room was under constant surveillance, and everything was being recorded. Thank goodness. Proof to the rest of the staff that this was not a nice man; this was a psychopath.

My hand was still gripped around the phone and I waved it around. "I'm calling the cops."

Murdoch shrugged. "Go ahead. I've done nothing wrong."

And that was true. Bastard had me on a goddamn technicality. *Today* he'd done nothing wrong. Forty-eight hours ago, he had. Now it made no sense that I hadn't pressed charges or at least filed for a restraining order, I could've prevented this jerk from entering the school, not that it would've stopped him. He'd already broken the ban.

Murdoch took another step toward me and I feared that my heart would burst free from its bony cage. "Miss Evans…" Two feet separated me from him. Twenty-four inches of barely breathable air. He could reach out and grab me if he wanted.

"Step away from her." Wentworth advanced on Murdoch's left but refrained from grabbing him. Why wasn't he hauling him out of here? Why were they just standing there?

I wanted to look at Liam, but I feared for my safety if I pried my eyes off Murdoch. The man looked possessed; the strangest desire lurked in the depths of his eyes. A Cheshire grin spread wickedly across his bearded face.

Things would not bode well if he got any closer.

"I just want to talk."

Why was he repeating that over and over? As if. I didn't want to talk and I sure as hell didn't want to be his friend. The words coming from him were all lies and everyone in this room knew it. His back was to the camera, but I didn't miss the grotesque way he licked his lips.

However, I didn't give him the satisfaction of looking away. Instead, with more hatred than I've ever felt fueled through my body, I glared at him. "No!" I jerked my left hand up. "Back off!" If no one was going to make a move on him until he made one on me, this was going to be a long afternoon. There was no way he was getting any closer.

Instantly, he grabbed my arm and yanked me against his chest.

It was the moment I needed. In a quick motion, recalling a movie scene I watched years ago, I slammed the pointy heel of my shoe into his foot and followed through by driving my elbow into the wall of his chest as

I spun around. "I SAID BACK OFF!" I stepped back and stared at him. "GET OUT OF MY WAY!"

Not messing around, he stepped off to the side grunting and gasping for breath, and in a heartbeat, I pushed by him and made my way into the staff room. My feet barely carried me over to the sofa chair before I collapsed.

Grunts and swears permeated the vacated air I'd left behind, but I tried to pay it no attention. I pulled my legs under me and curled my head into my knees, tears falling fast and hard down my cheeks and soaking through my pantyhose.

Liam shuffled in and made his way over to where I was, sitting on the sofa's armrest. His hand softly touched the space between my shoulder blades.

I shook my shoulders and pulled away. "Don't touch me, please." It came out in a sob; a weak, soul-crushing sob. So much of me desired being held in his arms, but the smaller part—the stronger part—craved the emotional and physical isolation needed to process. "He's going to just keep coming back, isn't he?"

Liam dragged one of the standard chairs over, sitting within inches of me but respecting the boundary I'd popped up. "At this point, legally we can't keep him away. His daughter attends school here."

"And if I press charges, for Monday, or file a restraining order?"

"Then you wouldn't need to worry about him moving forward."

But I'd have to retell my version of the events. Be in the spotlight and questioned about my actions, my reactions, things I said and did. It would be me against him as there were no cameras. And only one witness. "You'd have to give a statement too." I peered at him while tipping my cheek onto my knee.

"I know."

"You're okay with that?"

"If it helps you out, I'm all over it."

I righted my head, digging my chin into my knee. Some would say it was an easy choice. I thought it was an impossible one. Would I be believed? Would Liam? How would retelling his version make him feel? Would I get a sympathetic cop to hear my side without judging, or would I get the jerk who would already be blaming me because I didn't say no? I made sure to say no today though. And it's on camera, although Murdoch's facial expressions are hidden. Could they prove intent from that?

But it would keep me away from him. That was a plus. How would that affect Lily though? Would she need to be transferred? If Murdoch was banned from stepping on the premises, how would Lily get safely home? And if she did transfer, would Murdoch try to attack another teacher at the new school?

There were so many questions, none of which I had the answers to but as selfish as it was, I had to protect myself.

I sighed and put my feet on the floor. Time to face the music. "I'll give a statement to the police and file for a restraining order."

Chapter Nineteen

$\mathcal{I}$ was proud to say I got through giving my statement with little emotion. I was sure the investigating officer thought I was dead inside, but I kept it to the facts and the facts alone. Emotion didn't even enter the equation. That would come out later, no doubt, and would be properly tampered down with a glass of whatever I could find. Damn Trey for taking my bottle of whiskey. My funds were running low, and I couldn't keep affording running the liquor store.

"We're good now?" I asked Officer Khan.

"Yes, ma'am. You're free to go." She passed me her card and tapped the number on the back. "Call them and they'll expedite your restraining order against Mr. Murdoch."

"Is he out there?" When the police arrived, I was shuffled into the VP's office, and Murdoch was still folded under the watchful eye of Wentworth, in the main part of the office.

"He's been charged and taken in for processing."

A wave of relief washed over me. It thrilled me to know I'd likely never see him again, and although I had surprised him—and myself—with my defensive manoeuvres, a part of me was glad I hadn't done any permanent damage. Officer Khan was pleased that I had been able to defend myself, but I was shocked. I'd never struck another person in my life.

"And what will happen with Lily, and her sister?" The bell was about to ring. Someone needed to pick them up.

"I heard an aunt is coming to get them."

Poor Lily. Probably horrified and confused at watching her father escorted out in cuffs. Hopefully, there was some sort of service they'd provide her to help her deal with what went down. And where was Edalyn, the nanny?

I rose out of the chair and shook my hands to discharge the pent-up energy I had. The adrenaline had finally ghosted its epic battle, and all that was left was the shakes and dizzying letdown.

The officer opened the door and the hum of a regular afterschool frenzy floated into the space. Parents questioning the police cars and asking the officers if their children were in any danger. It was a little distressing, but I understood their concern. It would ignite curiosity in me too if I saw officers lingering around. Thankfully the bad guy in question was no longer present and represented no danger to the students or other staff members.

Officer Khan returned. "Your principal's requesting that you stay here until the activity out there dies down."

Well, I wasn't about to go strolling down the hallway, but I did want to find Liam. Still, I nodded at her and sat down, grabbing a paper clip from off the desk. I straightened it and attempted to bend it back into shape. It was fruitless, all it did was look completely messed up. I sympathized with the paper clip. No matter what I did to return it into what it was, there was always a kink that wouldn't conform. Always a little misshapen despite the best efforts. I tossed the metal across the desk and rested my heavy head against the wall.

The wall separating the principal's office from the VP's were a little thicker than paper. But not much. From the other side, I distinctly heard Liam's voice. And it was cracking.

Hearing the emotion in his voice, destroyed me on a level I'd never knew existed. It propelled me out of my chair, through the door and three steps to the open door where another officer sat beside Liam, furiously scribbling down notes.

Liam locked his red-rimmed gaze on me. He swiped a hand across his eyes and returned his focus to the officer.

It broke my heart to see him in such turmoil. I stepped around the officer and fell on my knees in front of Liam, touching his thighs. "Oh, I'm so sorry for all of this."

"You don't get to be sorry." Those dark eyes of his had become even darker, if that were even possible, but they held me in the tenderest hold.

"But I am. I'm sorry I didn't get a restraining order on Monday. I'm sorry you had to see that. I'm sorry–"

His finger covered my lips. "You need to stop apologizing right now. You did nothing wrong."

"But if I-"

"Stop." His voice came out stronger than I think he expected, and he recoiled at the sound of it. "Please, Camille, just stop trying to help everyone deal with what happened. We were just witnesses," he shuddered, "but you were the victim."

A gag threatened to announce itself. "Can you please never use that phrase again?" I hated that word. It

186

had such a negative connotation to it, as if the person who had just experienced something awful was somehow weak and loser-ish. If it was one thing I wasn't, it was a loser. And after attacking Murdoch, weak shouldn't be a phrase I'd be associated with either. However, that 'V' word, it instantly changed people's perceptions and I'll be damned if I wanted that thrown at me.

"But you are."

"Maybe according to the dictionary." I rolled my eyes and pushed down the ill feelings swirling around in my gut. "But I don't want to discuss that right now. I'm concerned about you, and what you're feeling and experiencing right now." My fingers squeezed his knee and he placed his hand upon it.

"I'll be okay." He sniffed and with his free hand reached for a tissue.

"You don't look it." I reached up and wiped away a freshly formed tear.

Liam folded more into himself. "It just bugs me what that creep did and what he could've done."

"But he didn't. And I'm so thankful for that." The thought of all the could have beens, it was enough to produce the vilest of nightmares. What would've happened that day had Liam not shown up? I wasn't sure where my room ranked on the cleaning list; it could've been hours later before Wentworth came by. Who knew?

"And I worry about what this is doing to you. I worry that you'll internalize it more than you'll vocalize it and I don't want that." His eyes focused on mine, and with it, I sensed a depth of longing. Like the last thing he ever wanted was to see the suffering and he'd rather be dragged into and be a part of it than watch from the sidelines.

"I'm absolutely positive you don't want to hear my every waking thought on it." That level of self-hatred wasn't a suicidal level, but it would be enough to rattle the most confident.

"That's where you're wrong. I don't want you to go downhill like..."

"Your wife did." And I understood that. "I can promise you, if I am feeling that low, I will let you know."

That perked him up a bit. "Promise?"

"Cross my heart." The words *'and I hope to die'* almost rolled out afterwards, but I bit my tongue before they could.

He tapped my hand twice before squeezing it. "Are we all done?"

In that personal moment, I'd totally forgot that someone else was in the room. I cleared my throat and twisted back to look at the officer.

"We're good." He produced a card and scribbled

on it. "If you think of anything else, this is my direct line."

"Thank you." Liam rose and helped me onto my feet. He then shook the officer's hand. "Thanks for responding so quickly."

The policeman put his hat on and walked out into the main part of the office, leaving Liam and me alone in Saunder's office.

"Are you okay?" I asked. He'd lost a little colour since standing.

"Are you?"

"Yeah, actually. In spite of everything, I'm okay. He didn't get what he wanted today." I believed the words as I spoke. "Are you going to manage?"

He gave me a soft nod and linked his fingers through mine. I grabbed on tighter, no instinct to twist away or turn from him. It felt comfortable and natural, and it kept me in the moment, not wondering what lay waiting beyond the door. All I wanted to do was stay in the space and share it with Liam.

"I don't know about you, but I sure could use a–"

A knock sounded against the door jam.

Wentworth stood in the doorway, with his arms crossed over his chest. "How are you both doing?"

I broke away from Liam. A moment ago, I'd been ready to have him wrap his arms around me and hug me.

Hold me tight and keep me from physically falling apart. Instead, my feet moved me over to Wentworth. "Thank you. For everything with…"

"S'all good." He waved through the air.

"Yes, thank you." Liam came over and shook his hand.

I stared at Wentworth, who towered over me. "Please know I'm grateful for all you did."

He blinked a few times but never moved. "I think I should explain why I wasn't making a move on Murdoch."

I stretched myself taller to take it in. It was a question I'd taken a millisecond to ponder.

"He needed to make the first move, otherwise I'd be the one charged for throwing the first punch. And I was watching his every move, his every twitch. When he grabbed your hand, I was right there ready to take him down, but you managed to knock him out." He winked, and a proud smile blossomed across his face. "Well done."

"It's nothing I'm proud of, but thanks."

"Since I'm done here, I'm going home to have a beer with my wife. See you tomorrow?"

"I'll be here."

Wentworth bid us adieu and walked into the main part of the office, chatting up the few remaining people.

Liam stood protectively close to me as I stared

down the hall. "Where'd you learn that move, by the way?"

"You'll laugh if I tell you." Because it sounded silly, but it's amazing what pops into my head at the wrong, and sometimes right, moment.

"Try me."

I sucked in my breath. "Miss Congeniality. I did it out of order though."

"Remind me to send a note of thanks to Sandra Bullock." He wrapped his arm around my shoulders. "Can I take you home?"

Nothing would've made me happier, but I had a dinner date with Trey. Tonight was going to be the night I cut the ties that bound us together. With any luck, it would end with us still being friends. "I'd like that."

"I hear a but."

"I have things to set straight with Trey."

His arm tensed but he didn't drop it. "Oh right. That."

"He had a new friend last night, so this is something I should've done a long time ago." It's not like I was jealous, because nothing could be further from the truth. Our relationship was not a typical one.

"Hey," Liam said, touching my chin and tipping it up. He stared into my eyes. "There you are." A small smile tickled the edges of his lips. "Call me later? Let me know how it goes."

My shoulders cooled as he removed his arm and thrust his hands into the pockets of his pants. Saunders had turned in our direction and headed toward us. Now that I had given my statement to the cops, it was time to fill in Saunders so he could inform the staff. I inhaled a deep breath of courage and readied myself for the inquisition.

Chapter Twenty

My meeting with Saunders was much quicker than expected. Rather than a long process of probing questions, he asked if I was okay and if he should contact our mental health department and set up a few meetings with them. It was unexpectedly nice, and before I gave it much thought, I found myself agreeing. Oh well. It was paid for.

As I opened the stairwell door in my apartment building, I was surprised to see Trey standing dressed like he was heading to a sporting event.

"There you are. I was just about to send out a search party." He raised his phone to show me that although his tone was joking, his words were sincere.

"It's been a long day."

He rolled his eyes. "What else is new?"

"Seriously. It was another day of cops and statements."

That wiped the condescending look off his face. "Seriously? Did a parent go postal? Did a student?" He flipped through his phone.

"It's not newsworthy and you won't find it on Twitter."

He dropped his hand, fingers still wrapped tightly around his phone.

My hand froze as I inserted the key into the lock. Pounding palpations beat through me and a cold sweat lurked on the edge of my shirt along the nape of my neck. "However, it is something we need to talk about. Desperately."

Once inside, I locked the door and dropped my bag by it. "I need a drink. Want one?" I rummaged through the cabinet and found a bottle of vodka with enough liquor in it to fill half a glass. It would have to do. Trey shook his head. I downed my glass and pushed the bottles around until I found another bottle with an ounce in it. Time to go shopping and put it on the credit card. I was pretty sure the cut off had happened, and I wouldn't need to worry about paying the bill until the end of next month.

"Fine," Trey removed the bottle from my hand.

"You've had your drink. That's enough for now."

"You're no fun." It was supposed to come out with a snicker, but it rolled out with a punch instead.

"Anyways…" Trey grabbed me by the hand and lead me over to the couch. Holding his hand wasn't like threading my fingers through Liam's. There was something way different. Almost forced. How many times had we actually held hands? Flipping through recent memories, we didn't. It wasn't our thing. We weren't a couple who showed our affection that way. We didn't show affection in any way.

I pulled my hand away and rubbed my forearms. "Do you want the sugar-coated version or the hit you between the eyes version?"

He shrugged. "The truth is best."

"Fine. Where to start?" I could go back years, or to last week, or start with today and go back in time. "I attacked a parent today." My filter failed. Guess I was starting today and moving backwards through time.

Trey burst out laughing, so not the reaction I expected. "Wow. I know you are hardcore about your students, but geez."

"He attacked me." I gulped down a morsel of fear. Murdoch wasn't going to win anymore. "On Monday. He touched me here." My hand fell on my left boob and thankfully my heart rate only rose a little. I was still in control. "And here." My other hand covered my lap. It didn't take long for the memory of the violent hand grab to surface. Closing my eyes, I breathed in deeply and counted to ten.

Trey's voice fell. "Is it too late to ask for the sugar-coated version?"

"That was." I opened my eyes.

"Shit, Cammy. I don't know what to say." He ran his hand through his hair. Clearly, he'd been working the fryers since his hair stayed slicked back and didn't fall nicely over his forehead in that charming way it once used to.

I played with the hem of my skirt, running my nails along it. "Last week, he kept asking me out, and I kept turning him down. Friday, he made a move on me which conjured some bad memories I couldn't properly deal with."

While Trey held his breath, a pensive look sewed his brows together into a tight line. "Well, that finally explains Friday. You scared me that night."

"I'm sorry, that wasn't my intention. I was in a bad place."

"The alcohol probably didn't help."

A huff breezed out of me. "It actually made it

easier to deal with. All I could see was his face."

"That parent guy from school?"

"Yes, him and…" I stopped. That can of worms wasn't to be opened. Ever. Some memories were like icebergs. Just seeing the tip of the ice was enough. No point in uncovering the full depth of the horror. "Anyway…"

"And you punched him out today in revenge?" Trey sported a smile.

"Yeah, but not revenge. More along the lines of self-defence. But I'm not proud of it."

"I sure am. Look at my girl."

"Trey, I think you're missing the point. I didn't go looking to attack him."

"No, no, I get that." He slapped his knee. "I'll remember not to piss you off."

I sighed, long and hard, while staring at the man across from me. "Are you serious?"

"About?"

"Your attitude about this? I'm sharing something deeply personal, and you're seeing only the violence I dished out, not any of the lead up to what caused it."

"Violence?" He cocked an eyebrow and pressed his back into the couch, propping his foot on his knee. "You defended yourself, you said so yourself. Hardly."

197

"He attacked me. Unprovoked. Sexually." My voice was starting to rise, and I needed to regain control. Trey wasn't supposed to be a target of my anger.

"I get that."

"Do you?" I wasn't expecting him to fall over with concern but was it too much to ask for a little sympathy?

He rolled himself forward and clasped his hands together. "Sorry. Let me rephrase." Long fingers rubbed his five o'clock shadow. "Let me see if I can reword this. This parent has been hitting on you for some time. You turned him down and he attacked you... and touched you." His hand waved up and down my body. "He went to do it again, and you laid a ghetto beating on him. Is that right?"

I tipped my head and tensed my hands into tight little fists. "I didn't beat him up. I elbowed him in the chest and dug my high heel into his foot."

"What am I missing? You're mad at me, but I can't figure out why. I didn't do anything."

"How about some god-damned sympathy?"

He threw his hands into the air and rolled into the couch. "Good gawd, Cammy. I've tried giving you sympathy. You shot me down. Every fucking time. I asked you to let me in, and you shut me out further. Were you going to let me in on Friday night?"

"I was battling a few ghosts."

198

"I know. Thus the reason I wanted to help. Remember, I sat outside the door all night, watching over you as best as I could."

My gaze fell into my lap, my anger dissipating as it did. "That was sweet of you."

"I know, right?" His head bobbled quickly. "And last night, were you going to tell me what was going on?"

I threw my hands up. "Fine. You want to know? I drank too much and fell asleep in the tub."

His jaw nearly hit the floor. "Jesus Christ, Cammy. That's dangerous. You could've drowned."

I shook my head, rage rearing its ugly head once again. "*That* you get angry about? For-fucking-real?"

"I don't want you dead." He rolled his eyes.

My nails dug into my palms. A little harder and they'd break the skin. I gritted my teeth and squeezed. "I don't get you, I really don't."

"Same."

Like I'd been zapped, I stood and marched into my kitchen, flexing my fingers and staring at the half-moon shapes carved into my skin. Twisting off the cap to the only liquor bottle I had left, I tipped my head back and drained it, inserting my tongue to make sure I got every last ounce. Sadly, there was nothing left.

"Cammy."

"Just stop, okay? Save me the speech and your pity." I glared at him and slammed the bottle onto the counter. "You know what, we're done."

"Done?"

"Yeah, like over. No more whatever the hell we are. We're not exclusive and haven't been for a very long time. I'm sick of being some side action when you can't find someone else." After rolling the bottle out of the way, I braced myself against the countertop and dug my toes into the carpet, preparing for a launch.

Trey just stood there like a statue. He lost the ability to even blink. "We're over?"

"I can't do this anymore. I can't keep you at arm's length from my problems and when I reel you in to share it with you, you push back against the idea. Clearly, our future together is not..." What? It wasn't romantic. That ship sailed a long time ago. Sexy? The urge to jump his bones and scream into my pillow had disappeared like a fart in the wind. It'd been more like scratching an itch than anything deeper. It wasn't lovemaking, it was sex. Pure and simple. And right now, that wasn't what I needed. I needed something deeper.

"What is it you want from me?"

I turned my face toward him, my shoulders rolling inward. What I needed was companionship. Friendship even, but we weren't connecting on the right level to make that happen. We'd been together, in a sense, for eight months, and yet I knew more about Liam and his life than I did about Trey. I'd learned more about Liam in a few days than I had about the one I'd been calling my boyfriend. "I honestly don't know. Doesn't that say something?"

The wind was out of his sails too. His shoulder connected with the wall and he leaned into it. "I don't know, I guess."

"I love you but in a way that's not romantic. Does that make sense?" In my head, it was perfectly clear.

"I can change."

I sighed and took a long hard look at Trey. He was a decent guy with a good heart, most of the time. Pretty good looking, average smarts. But he didn't light a fire in me. I didn't get excited to see him. And the worst part was I hadn't in a long time. That feeling of butterflies had faded very quickly. "You and I both know that's not healthy. I don't want you to change. You're the right person for someone, just not me." It sounded harsher than I wanted, but it was the truth. Maybe that Charla person was his special someone, or maybe, in some weird way, I'd been holding him back and that person was still out there.

He puffed out his chest and stepped closer to me.

"Is it that other guy? Liam, was it?"

"I don't know. Maybe." I didn't want to get my hopes up. "He's a good guy."

"I gathered that." He rested his hand over top mine. "You deserve someone good."

I stared deeply into his eyes. "So, do you. Whoever she is, she's out there waiting for you. And maybe she'll even enjoy a good Nic Cage flick." I didn't understand his obsession with that man. The only movie I saw with him in it that was half-way decent was *National Treasure*.

Trey shrugged. "Maybe." Sadness laced his features. "So, if we're done, does that mean we'll never see each other again?"

"Would that make it easier on you?" My heart stopped for a breath. As much as I didn't want to be tangled up with Trey, I still wanted to be friends. Just not friends with benefits.

He shook his head. "Not at all."

Relief washed over me. "Whew. Me either."

"We really do have a weird relationship."

"We do, but I think we'll be stronger as friends." At least I hoped. He opened his arms giving me what I needed, and I didn't pass on the opportunity. I rested my head against his chest. "I still love you, you know."

"I know." He kissed the top of my head and

tightened his hold on me.

He'd never said it. Implied it lots, but those three words had never left his mouth. It cemented for me that I was doing the right thing by cutting him loose. Clearly, we weren't meant to be. There was someone that perhaps I was meant to be with. Time would tell.

Chapter Twenty One

*A*fter a lingering embrace where neither of us spoke, Trey was the first to physically break us apart.

"I should go." His face was devoid of expression. Maybe my breaking up with him did affect him on a deeper level than I understood.

"Okay." I didn't feel as strong as I hoped, and I think that came out in my tone.

"You'll be alright?"

My shoulders rose and fell. "It's what I want."

"If you ever need me…"

"I know where to find you." I forced a small smile on my face. Every other break up I'd been a part of had been an angry, heat of the moment destruction. This was a slow fade. Almost as if it was tinged in remorse and regret. But it wasn't. However, neither of us wanted to actually leave.

He stood by the door and unlocked it, pulling it open and flooding the kitchen with the brightest lights to ever grace a hallway. "Maybe on the weekend, we can grab dinner together?"

"I'd like that."

"Me too." He stepped out into the hallway.

I put my hand on the doorknob and waited. I wanted him to walk away before I closed the door, to accept that this was mutual, but he continued to stand there.

"What about your things?"

Unsure what objects of mine would be in his place, I tried remembering what might possibly be there. Most of our hookups had been in my apartment and the walk of shame was truly a quick flight of stairs. "Bring them to dinner."

"Will do." He stepped away, inching his way to the stairwell door. "Have a good night."

Wasn't sure what good would come out of it, but I knew he was just being polite. "You too, Trey." Hopefully, he had a number in his phone that he could dial and release a little of his feelings on. Maybe that would put a spring back in his step.

"See ya."

He was enough out of sight that I didn't feel guilty

about closing the door and securing the locks in place. It was done. I'd ripped the proverbial bandage off, and the wound underneath was in better shape than I expected. I hated seeing him so dejected, but this was the right decision. Now he could go about his floundering ways without it affecting me. I didn't have this weird relationship to be aware off, I was free myself to do whatever I wanted. Which at the moment, wasn't much.

I wanted a drink, but I was out. My cupboards were dry. After a quick check on the funds in my bank account, I hopped into my car and drove to the liquor store. Time to refill my supply.

Well damn. I got a sale and bought three bottles of booze: one each of vodka, whiskey, and rum. The three musketeers. Perfect.

I placed the bottles in their new homes and debated which I needed most tonight. The rum had been a total impulse purchase as I'd never had a spiced version, but I did like a good fireball whiskey, so it couldn't be too bad.

I twisted the lid off and sniffed. Smelled decent. Searching through the cupboard, all four of my glasses were dirty. Fuck it. I carried the bottle into the living room and sat on the sofa, putting the bottle on the table in front of me after a quick swig. Damn, it burned more than I thought it should. But it was a good burn.

My phone buzzed and I gave it a quick pass. An email to the staff from the principal regarding new safety measures which would be discussed at a staff meeting already scheduled for tomorrow at recess. I didn't envy his position and was sure Saunders had a long evening ahead of him. The school board was involved which likely only increased the amount of paperwork he'd need to do. There were plenty of reports he needed to provide and thinking about it all made me tired.

My thoughts drifted away. To a simpler time. To Mexico. I wanted to go back. Maybe move there permanently and set up camp right on the beach. Tess had entertained that thought, not as much as I had though. I really should update her on what the hell was going on in my life. As my best friend, she was entitled to know. I didn't have to tell her about the deeply personal stuff, just about him. And how Liam was with it. And how Trey wasn't quite as sympathetic as I'd wanted? Hoped? Ah, it didn't matter. He was gone now.

My thumb hovered over Tess's name. I quickly typed out, *had a shitty day. Actually, a shitty week. Can we get together?*

She was quick. *Give me five.*

While I waited for her response, I took another drink. It went down smoother than the first one, so I filled my mouth with it. Swallowed it down in about three gulps. The tips of my fingers started to tingle. Finally.

Tess typed. *What's up?*

Can you come over? I've been drinking and can't drive.

Be right there.

Tess lived a few blocks away, but the way our roads were designed, it would take less time to walk on the paths between us than it would be to drive and find parking.

In ten minutes, my door buzzed, and Tess was on her way up.

She was all lit up, sporting a radiant glow on the apples of her cheeks, and it wasn't from the jog over. That girl was in love and she had it bad.

"What's up?"

"Sit. I have a lot to tell you."

Her eyes widened as she closed the door and followed me over to the couch.

I sat on one end and crossed my legs. For good measure, I took another drink and twisted the lid back on.

Her phone buzzed, and she looked at it.

"Go ahead and answer it."

"I promise I'll be quick." Her smile widened. "Hi, honeycakes."

Ugh. When had they graduated to disgustingly cute pet names? With the bottle firmly in my hand, I excused the couple and went to the bathroom. Their gaganess went on and on, so I shut the door and took a quick leak. My face had lost its perkiness and I pinched a bit of colour into my cheeks. It lasted for a moment before it washed away. The bottle of rum called out my name, and wanting to keep at least one thing happy, I obeyed and put it in my mouth, swallowing everything I could in a few seconds. Success. I slammed the bottle down and wiped my mouth with the back of my hand.

Slowly, I opened the door and listened. The two of them were still going back and forth. Screw it. It was my place and I invited her over. I wobbly marched into the living room and flopped down on the couch.

"Say hi to Jon." She flashed her phone in my direction.

"Hi," I said when I saw his face. He had a sort of cuteness to him that was adorable. Maybe it was the way he treated Tess that brought it out. Whatever it was, he was good to her and treated her with respect and love. He didn't cheat on her like Trey did with me, and I think if Tess and Jon broke up, Jon would actually be devasted. Unlike Trey, who was sad but not crushed.

Tears built and blurred my focus on Jon, but I waved regardless.

"You okay, Camille?"

"No. That's why Tess came over."

I crawled over and rested my head in Tess's lap, like I used to in high school. Tess responded the way I'd hoped and started stroking my hair.

"I'll call you later and see you in thirty-three hours." She hung up as he said goodbye. She had plans to spend the weekend with him. "What's going on? And how much have you had to drink?"

"Whatever's missing from the bottle."

"And where is the bottle?"

It was on the table, but then I took it with me. "Bathroom?"

"Are you asking me or telling me?"

"Nope, it's in there." It was sitting all alone on the counter, next to the soap. "Trey and I broke up."

"Oh dear." She finger-brushed through my hair. It felt so calm, I could've stayed there forever. "Is that why you're upset?"

"Partially. It's been a long week. Today, I punched out a parent who attacked me on Monday."

"You what?" Tess pushed me into a sitting

position. "What the hell is going on?"

The sudden movement sent my head into a death-defying spin and I put my hands on my head to stop the motion. "Easy, T-bird." When I felt the tornado slow down, I spit out all the details and wasted no time in doing so. The more I told, the faster the words came out, until it was nearly verbal diarrhea spewing all over her. I'll give her credit though; she took the news worse than Trey. It actually turned her green. That was the empathetic part of her though. She took every emotion so personally. It was a good thing Liam wasn't in the room when I told the story, she'd probably keel over from absorbing all the negativity.

"I need some air." She raced over to the patio door and cracked it, sticking her nose out into the fresh air. A few good gulps, she returned the couch. "That's better." Never one to shy away from touching me, she pulled me into her arms. "What can I do to help you? Do you need to stay at my apartment?"

"I'm not worried about being here."

"What about school? Is Liam taking care of you?"

The conversation we had in the principal's office, the deep feelings he had over the situation because of what his wife went through, and how protective he'd become, they all spilled out in a rapid pace.

"He sounds like a keeper."

"He's a good guy. And I really like him."

"Good. I've always said you need to find someone better than Trey. He's nice and all, but he's not the guy for you. If he was, you'd know it deep in your heart."

"Then why do I miss him so?"

"Trust me, it's not Trey you're missing."

I raised an eyebrow. How? "Explain."

"It's the idea of him. Just like when I broke up with Filipe. I missed the idea of having someone to cuddle with and share my day to day with."

"You have me."

She laughed, a light and airy sound. "Yes, this is truth but as much as I love you, you're not my soul mate."

"And Jon is?" They'd only been a couple for a month, if that. It couldn't be that serious.

A bashful expression filled her face and lit up her eyes. "Maybe. I think so. Yes."

"And he's on board with that?"

"He's trying to figure out a way for us to be together. Where we'd live, what we'd do for jobs." She sighed, lost in dreamy thoughts.

Wow. I was both impressed and saddened by this. As happy as I was for Tess, because no one deserved true happiness more than she did, I couldn't imagine my T-bird living anywhere that wasn't a ten-minute walk away.

"But it's not going to happen anytime soon, so you can wipe away your worries. Besides, I need to see this thing between you and Liam to its final conclusion."

"And what conclusion would that be? We haven't even really started." Because once he found out about Trey, that whole idea was squashed until I ended it.

"How long have I known you, Camille? Fifteen, sixteen years?"

"Yeah, something like that."

"In all that time, have you ever been in love?"

True love? Probably not, but there was that quasi-love I thought I had with Ronin back in college. Didn't know until after we ended things that it was all lust and no love. Even Trey had been a quasi-type of love. All hype though, and very little substance. "I see what you're doing, but I'm not in love with Liam."

"Not now, but in Mexico, you looked at him in a way I've never seen you with a guy. Not as someone you'd hook up with, because there was lots of that going on."

Why did that sound like a tsking coming from her?

"But you looked at Liam as an equal, and from what I've seen, I think you two are evenly matched. A true partnership. When you're both ready for it."

"Yeah, well, I don't know when that will be. Likely never." He was right though. I had to have some perspective on things and make sure I was dumping Trey for the right reasons, and that I was ready to move on to someone else, possibly him, when I was ready for it and not because my bed was cold or I was emotionally lonely. Lately, my bed has been very cold, and I truly couldn't get lonelier on an emotional level if I tried.

"You're too hard on yourself."

"What?" And this was what I meant about Tess. I didn't even have to say anything, she just sensed what was going on in my head. Another reason why I couldn't bear it for her to move away from me. Tess just understood me.

I placed my head on her lap and rubbed her leg. The alcohol was making me heavy and sleepy. "Tess?"

"Yeah?"

"Do you really think Jon's the one?"

She twirled my hair in her fingers. "I do."

"Even only knowing him for such a short time?" She only knew him five days longer than I knew Liam, but with all the working hours I had with Liam, I was sure in terms of spending actual time with the person, that I was further ahead. And I liked Liam. I trusted him.

"Yeah." There was no hesitation in her voice. "I have a feeling the future is going to be so amazing. And so will yours be."

"It has nowhere to go but up."

Chapter Twenty-Two

L iam pulled into the parking lot at the same time as I did, however, his parking stall was three away from mine, so I hung out beside my car and waited for him.

"You never called last night, how'd it go?" He always dressed so nicely. A healthy mix of professional yet casual.

My dress was a step up from my usual. Instead of a cotton dress, this was a silky one with a lining. The dark colour went well with my navy pumps. "It was hard, and then I called my girlfriend Tess over. She was the one from the lounge."

"To nurse your wounds?" He slung his bag over his shoulder and stayed in step beside me.

Obviously, Liam thought more about Trey and I's relationship then there was. "No. Maybe. I needed my best friend last night. Yesterday was a very long day. In fact, it's been a long a week."

"I can't argue with that." He buzzed us into the school and held the door open for me to enter ahead of him.

I put a little more sashay into my step, thinking he might be watching. I waved at the secretary in the office and walked down the long hallway to my room.

"So, you and Trey are done?"

Ignoring his question and since I was first to arrive, I unlocked my door and then crossed the hall to do the same to his, pulling it open for him.

"Drop your bag off and we'll go grab coffee."

In my oversized purse, there was a travel mug of coffee, but I didn't have the heart to tell Liam. After last night's restless sleep, I needed something with a little more kick. My regular breakfast shake wasn't strong enough. A minute later, I stood by my door waiting for him.

He came out of his room holding a mini bouquet of wildflowers, not from a field but from a floral shop. An expensive one. "These are for you."

"Wow. Thanks." In all my life, I'd never been the recipient of flowers from a guy. I'd received dandelions and the like from students, but that was completely different. "They're nice." I nuzzled my nose into the ribbon-wrapped bouquet. "Is there lavender in here?"

"Could be?" He winked. "Put them beside your

bed. It should help you sleep a little bit better."

"Thank you. They're lovely."

"It's just a little something to let you know I'm thinking of you."

Heat blossomed over my cheeks and I spun around to head to my desk to avoid him seeing the change in colouring. Somewhere on my desk was a water bottle. Spying it, I quickly hacked at the neck of it with a pair of scissors to make it wider and dropped the stems into it. By the time that was done, the heat had softened, and I was ready to make an appearance in the staff room for coffee.

"All ready, Miss Evans?"

"As ready as ever, Mr. Donaldson."

He seemed like he was ready to take my hand, but at the last minute changed his mind. Probably best as we needed to keep things strictly professional on school grounds. Company policy.

He kept step with me down the hall, even when my steps became shorter with hesitation. Gossip was not uncommon, but as much as I hoped the whole thing would not be a topic of conversation, that thought was laid to rest. When I walked into the staff room, the murmurs stopped, and the staff members all stared at me.

"Hey," I said and tossed my shoulders back while walking over to the coffee machine.

Someone, I don't know who, started clapping, and within seconds the staff room was ringing with cheers.

"We heard you kicked ass."

"You sure showed him."

"That guy was such a creep."

The strangest and most sincere comment came from a thick-set woman, who taught the third grade. Daria, without warning, wrapped me in a hug and whispered in my ear that she wished she was as brave as I was. She stepped away and after filling her mug, left the room.

I wasn't brave. Far from it. Yesterday had been a fluke, and I had the opportunity to defend myself. That defence had been stripped from me on Monday when the whole thing happened without warning. I certainly wasn't brave then. I'd folded, and in some sort of sick self-preservation, I'd let it happen. Had there been even a small chance of escaping, I don't know that I would've been capable of leaving. Fear had kept me frozen to the ground.

A million questions came flying at me, and I didn't want to entertain their inquisitions.

My empty cup dangled from my fingertips. "I'm sorry. I just want coffee." And for the attention on this to die down. I liked attention as much as the next person, but this was too much. "Ask Wentworth." Liam had been quite disturbed by the whole thing; I wasn't about to throw him under the bus. Because I had nothing to be ashamed of, I added, "I'm sure if you ask Saunders, you can watch the video." I'd even be sort of curious to watch. It would be like having an out of body experience to see it from a different POV.

As I turned to the coffee pot, Liam handed me a cup full of dark liquid. "I don't know what you like in it."

"Just black, thanks." I stole a peek at his. Definitely milky. He didn't need to add any sweetener, he was plenty sweet already. I raised my mug to the staff who still watched my every move. "Have a great morning. See you at recess."

Like a bat out of hell, I marched as fast as possible to the sanctity of my room. Although my room wasn't as safe as it used to be. This had been the place of terror for a few minutes on Monday. That wall—that was where he cornered me and touched me and did things to me that made me scared and angry and sad and disgusted. He'd pinned my arms behind my back, he put his mouth on mine, he dominated me. His evil laugh floated through the air, piercing my heart and giving rise to the worst case of goosebumps ever.

"NO!" I screamed and covered my ears.

The laughter died down but his face was in front of me. Licking his lips. Lowering his lids with evil intent.

"STOP STARING AT ME!"

I lunged for the closest thing I could find – my mug of hot coffee, and I launched it with all my might at the wall. It shattered into a million pieces, breaking the image of his rotten snicker as a dark liquid sprayed in all directions.

Feeling trapped as someone wrapped their strong arms around me, I started pounding against his chest as I closed my eyes. "NO," I screamed at the top of my lungs.

"Camille, it's me." His voice was loud in my ears. "It's me. Open your eyes and look."

My vision was blurred with hot tears but through the haze, there was Liam's face.

"He's not here, I promise. You're safe. I've got you."

My next pound was softer, the fight gone in a heartbeat knowing it was Liam who held me. "I'm so sorry." I hadn't meant to hit him.

"You're safe." He pulled me in tighter, the heat from his arms warming the sudden chill running up and down the length of my back. "I've got you."

I stopped fighting, against both Liam and the impending war on my emotions. My legs gave out and I dropped to the floor, Liam beside me in a heartbeat. I curled against his chest and sobbed.

Chapter Twenty-Three

Liam

E scaping the women in the staff room was damn near impossible but somehow, I managed. All questions I directed to Saunders when he stepped into the room and once the first question flew out, I took my cue and abandoned ship. Not my finest moment, but I saw the despair brewing in Camille's eyes before she left. There was more going on inside her head than she was sharing, and she promised she'd share it with me. Neither of us had supervision at recess and I was determined that I was going to talk to her. No way was she going to handle this on her own.

Walking down the hall, a soul-crushing scream rolled out into the empty hallway.

"Stop staring at me."

My blood boiled instantly, and I worried that

somehow the freaking scumbag had snuck his way back into the school. I raced into her room just as a coffee cup went sailing through the air and smashed into the wall. Whatever she was seeing, it wasn't real, at least to me. But the ghosts were scaring the hell out of her.

In a heartbeat, I ran over to her and wrapped my arms around her. She felt so tense and tightly wound, and with it came a strength that hurt. Her fists pounded against my chest, knocking the breath from me.

"NO," she screamed at the top of her lungs. My ears rang from the intensity.

I needed to be firm but gentle. It's what Janet told me. "Camille, it's me." Controlling the strength of my voice wasn't hard, I'd learned it in musical training. I kept my tone even, but I needed her to not just hear me but listen to me too. In the state she was in, I doubted she heard anything. "It's me. Open your eyes and look."

Her beautiful brown eyes were filled with tears and peering deeper into them, haunted and withdrawn. She continued to wail on me, and damn it, her hits were strong. But it wasn't me she was attacking; I knew that much.

Instantly, I was enraged at Murdoch and the other man in her life who had scared her so badly and caused her so much pain and distrust. "He's not here, I promise." I lowered my voice and softened my tone, searching her to find the crack that would allow me in. "You're safe. I've got you."

Her pounding softened, and her voice withered. However, life fired behind her ghostly eyes. "I'm so sorry."

Damn her and her constant apologies. None of this was her fault. "You're safe." I wrapped her tighter, in part to stop her from hitting me, but mostly to keep her close. My hand rubbed her bicep. "I've got you. He's not here."

The fight left in an instant, and before I could grab her, she collapsed onto the rug. I dropped beside her and pulled her in, her body shaking with tears. The strength in her blew away and suddenly she was as fragile as fine china and I was slightly terrified to hold on to her too tightly, for fear she'd snap in half.

Janet told me that sometimes the strangest thing will set someone off, especially if they've been acting like everything is copasetic. And Camille had been acting like she was okay. Her walls were sky high, but right now, they'd crumpled around her, and I didn't want her cracking like Humpty Dumpty. I'd find the way to help put her back together, some way somehow.

I don't know if she felt their presence or not, but I sure did. I craned my neck at the two guests in the room, one of which was our vice principal and the other was her educational assistant.

Both tiptoed over, and Beverly, the VP, surveyed the shattered mug and the trail of exploded coffee. She shook her head and stared down at me.

Deep in my arms, Camille still sobbed.

"Get her out of here, take her to my office. Wentworth will clean the room before the kids come in." She glanced at her watch. "They'll have to go to your room while he finishes. The bell's going to go and it's best if the students don't see her like this."

I agreed. "Camille, we need to go."

She pulled on my shirt as I stood, and I practically lifted her onto her feet. Jesus, the girl was in rough shape. What was going on in her head?

Beverly gave her a friendly pat on the back, and she shirked away, pushing into me with a sob. Camille would've been horrified to see the pitiful look on Beverly's face and I'm glad she was buried into my chest.

Mrs. Barrie stood there with her hand over her mouth, trying yet failing to hide the shock of what she was seeing.

"She'll be fine," I said to her, praying that the words were truth.

I glanced up and down the hall. Only staff were around, mugs in hand, files and papers tucked under their arms. From my vantage point, I spotted three coming my way, the others were down another hallway.

Quickly, I escorted Camille down the long hall, which felt like something out of a horror movie. I swear it was never going to end, and actually felt like it was getting longer the more we walked it. How was that even possible?

I took her through the staff room, bypassing the front entrance where parents stood outside the door, and a chatting couple in the main office. We made it to Beverly's office, a place I'd become more familiar with over the last few days than I'd ever known in my life. Growing up, never once had I had a visit to the principal's office, and yet as a full-grown adult, here I was.

"Camille." I slipped her into the VP's chair. Of the three in the room, it was most comfortable.

She stared up at me, her expression without emotion. The sparkle in her eyes was gone and there was an emptiness there that scared me. I'd seen that look before.

Jane, the secretary, came to the door and looked in. Jumping over to her, I obstructed her view of Camille. "Is she okay?"

"No," I whispered. "Can you call in an emergency sub for her?"

With a quick nod, she was gone, and Beverly

showed moments later. She gestured for me to step out into the hallway with her, and I closed the door slightly. "I'm going to take her students until the sub arrives."

Did she hear me ask that of Janet? "Thank you. I know she'd be appreciative of that."

"We'll combine the two classes for now. I expect you back in your room shortly."

I'd been ready to fight that possibility. "With all due respect, I need to stay here. Camille needs me and trusts me."

Although Beverly was a good foot shorter than me, the intensity of her stare took me down a notch. She wasn't a woman to be messed with. A rigidness grabbed her by the shoulders, and it seemed like me staying with her wasn't going to be an option without a battle. Giving me a steely once over, she relaxed just enough that I thought I'd missed it. "Do you think she should go to the hospital?" Beverly peered around my shoulder to check on Camille.

"I hope we're not there yet. I think she just needs to process all that's gone on." And a quick phone call to my twin would yield more information on what would be absolutely best for her.

She shuffled on her feet. "It's the Easter long weekend, and early dismissal today." Her words not directed at me, but almost as if she was prioritizing things.

226

"Take her home. You'll both need a sub for the remainder of the morning. Keep me posted on her state of mind. If by Sunday she's still on edge, let me know and I'll book her a sub for the rest of the week."

Perfect. I had four days with her, VP approved. Not that I needed her permission, but it helped to know the admin was on my side with this.

"Leave when you think the hecticness of the morning has subsided. Around nine?"

I nodded. "She'll need her things…"

"I can gather those up for her." She turned to walk away.

"Beverly?"

The older woman turned around. "Yeah?"

"Thank you."

She nodded. "Take care of her."

I'd planned on it.

An hour later, I had her at her apartment.

"Can you pack a bag for the weekend?"

She looked at me like I was the one who lost their mind.

"You're going to come to my place for a few nights. Someplace you can unwind and relax in. Your every wish I'll cater to."

Maybe I misread her, because I was still getting the look like horns were growing out of my head. "I'll be okay here."

"Bullshit."

She stepped back.

"Listen, I know it sounds exceptionally forward, but with my car, I can't stay here. There's no charging port." I didn't want to have to explain the full technical aspect about the electric car, but it was better to have it parked in my garage and connected rather than sitting in a parking lot where vandals ran rampant. The sentry system on it would be running constantly as this neighbourhood wasn't the best.

"I don't know."

"I have a spare bedroom, and my parents cook a helluva mean Easter dinner. Do you have plans for Easter?"

"That's this weekend?"

I nodded in agreement. It really didn't feel like an upcoming holiday. "Do you have plans with your friend, Tess?"

"She's flying to Vegas for a weekend getaway with her boyfriend." Even her voice was lacking depth and emotion.

"So, you have no plans and I do." I tried to go for

cute and charming, but I think it came off stiff and creepy. "I'd love it if you'd be my date for dinner on Sunday."

A flash of hope lit behind her eyes, but it was gone just as quickly. "Sure."

I'd make sure, even if it sounded like a response you'd give the principal when he asked you to do something you'd rather not. "Did you want to go pack a bag?"

"Fine." She shuffled down the hall to her bedroom.

I pulled out my phone and fired off a quick text to my sister. She'd be at work, but I wondered if my idea would be helpful or push her away. I felt I was on the right track at the moment and clearly, Camille trusted me, especially if she was coming over for the weekend. That trust was crucial, and I was going to do everything I could to keep it safe and well protected.

I walked into her living room, shaking my head. A bottle of booze sat half full on the coffee table, an empty glass beside it. Hmm...someone had been drinking a bit. My legs carried me through the living room and into the kitchen. There on the counter, tucked off to the side was another bottle. This one was vodka, and beside it, an unopened bottle of whiskey. I knew she liked to drink and I'd seen her pour back the liquor before, but it seemed odd to me. Did she just enjoy the drink or was there more to it?

"I'm ready."

Her voice startled me, and I quickly set down the bottle, trying to act casual. "This is a good brand."

Her gaze fixated on the alcohol. "It's my favourite."

I hoped I heard the tone wrong, but it almost felt like there was more emotion in that statement than there had been in the limited conversation I'd had with her since her meltdown this morning.

"Let's go, shall we?" I extended my arm, and hesitantly, she looped her arm through it, shaking as she did.

I was on a quest now. A quest to prove to her that not all guys are scum. That she can trust me and to show her how much she was starting to mean to me.

Chapter Twenty-Four

This day was not going as planned. I was supposed to be working on bunny masks and decorating Easter eggs with my students, and instead, I was parked inside Liam's garage, sitting in his weird car. I couldn't even get out; I had to pull the latch and wait a sec so the windows could lower a bit before I pushed the door open. So bizarre.

Still, there was something sweet about the whole thing. Liam was at my door before it was fully ready and he held it open, giving me his hand and pulling me out.

His fingers wrapped through mine; soft and warm. We walked up the stairs into his house. It wasn't a modern built home but definitely newer than my apartment. One thing was clear as soon as I stepped into his place; this wasn't a house - it was a home. His furnishings weren't Goodwill rejects, and everything had a nice look to it. Not overly fancy, but comfortable and lived in. And something about being in it made me completely at ease.

I set my bag down by the back door and he immediately picked it up. "I'll show you where the spare room is." We walked through the kitchen and the living room and turned around a corner. "Bathroom. Sorry it's not a private one and the tub is really small. If you want to have a bath, just let me know and you can use the big one in my bedroom. Total privacy." He pushed open the door decorated in crisp whites and navy blues. "And for the weekend, your bedroom."

It was a little cooler in the room but was functional. A twin bed, a small dresser, and a bedside table. A few random pictures hung, and at a glance they looked old as they had barns and farm equipment in the foreground.

"My great-grandparents farm." He set my bag on the bed and rocked on his feet. "Mi casa et sous casa."

"What does that mean?"

"Anything here is yours as well. I want you to make yourself at home."

I wonder if he really did though because if I were at home, I'd be dressed down and having something to drink. Here I was a guest and I intended on acting properly.

"Are you thirsty? I don't think you had your coffee. I can even whip you up a pretty basic breakfast too?"

Ah no. I didn't manage to have even a sip before

I… well, before it went for a ride. "Coffee would be nice, thank you." I followed him into the kitchen, and he pointed out where everything was. Making quick mental notes, I gave him a nod as he popped a pod into his coffee pot and brewed a fresh cup. Even from where I stood, it had a nice scent. I meandered over to the sofa in the living room. It sunk as I flopped into it, but not in an old way, just in a thick, plushy way.

He brought over my coffee and set it on a coaster. "How are you doing?"

What a random question. "Fine."

Clearly, he read something into the confusion on my face and with a gentle laugh I enjoyed the sound of, he said, "We're in a safe place, free from distractions and intrusions." He sat beside me and rested his hand on my knee. "Are you interested in discussing what happened this morning, or would you rather not for the time being?"

My chin tipped down and my heart suddenly weighed a thousand pounds. I supposed I owed him an explanation; he'd been nothing short of kind. "Well, I… I don't know." Opening up to people was just not something I did. Anytime I had, it had been used against me. My gaze fell upon Liam's face. He was patient with me, and most importantly, he hadn't turned and ran. In getting comfortable, I pulled my legs under me and wrapped my arms around them. My voice lowered. "It was just a combination of everything, and I swear I heard his voice and I saw his face." Did he think strange of me for saying that? In that moment, Murdoch had been in my classroom, even if he really wasn't. "I'm not a mental case or anything like that."

"I never said you were." Long fingers, perfect for playing piano, rubbed his face. "I want to help you, however that may be. I'm a good listener, if you want to talk. If you just want to go for long walks, there's a beautiful lake just outside the city I can take you too. If you want to yell and scream, well, there's not much I can do for that." A smile broke across his face.

The urge to return it was strong, but it didn't make it to my lips. All of those things sounded wonderful, but I wasn't sure what I needed most, aside from a drink. Right now, the fact that he was sitting here with me and keeping me company was enough.

"Oh, and just a heads up before I forget, this is a dry house."

My eyebrow lifted in response to his comment. "A what?"

"There's no alcohol here. None. Even my vanilla extract is imitation." It was said with a hint of a laugh.

I failed to see the humour in it. "I'm not concerned

about that." Sure, it would be nice to have something fun to drink, but I didn't *need* it to get through the evening.

"I saw the bottles around your apartment."

Instantly, my blood pressure rose. "You were snooping?"

He threw his hands up in a stop manner. "Not at all. They were sitting out." He inhaled sharply and positioned himself closer. "How much do you consume nightly?"

"Are you accusing me of being an alcoholic because I enjoy having a shot or two?" Lifting myself up, I put some distance between us.

He shook his head. "I wasn't accusing."

"But you are, and telling me your house is dry made it sound like…" What was the word I was looking for? My mouth dried out like I'd shoved cotton into it.

"Listen, before you go and work yourself up, I was just letting you know that there are other ways of dealing with a problem."

I challenged his stare and talked in a low, firm voice. "I don't have a problem." I turned away from him and crossed my legs. What nerve. Invited me over to his place and trap me. Try to make it look like I have a drinking problem. Which I don't. I can stop drinking any time I want. I just happen to enjoy the taste of it. It's no worse than loving chocolate or fancy cars or reading books. My eyes narrowed in a scowl and I crossed my arms over my chest. This wasn't going well. I figured we'd hang out, have some fun together. Instead, it's turned into some kind of intervention.

Liam headed to the kitchen and made himself another coffee. In our tension-filled space, he drank all of his. "Would you like another?"

I shook my head. My coffee was still full, and likely cool enough to drink. "No, thank you."

"Fair enough." The machine ran and a fresh scent floated through the air. He sat on the far end of the couch. "Just so your friends don't think I've kidnapped you, I think you should let your buddy Tess know you're here, and maybe even that guy Trey."

It wasn't a bad idea, because at the moment I was feeling a little bit trapped, however, I also didn't feel like moving and fetching my phone from my purse. "I will later. Although Tess is gone, and Trey is likely still sleeping."

"Just so you know though…"

I braced myself.

"You're free to come and go."

"My car's at work."

"Fine," he smirked, "you tell me where you want to go, and I'll take you there."

"My own personal chauffeur." It had potential to be endearing in its sweetness, but I was still a little pissed about being labeled an alcoholic. I lifted the lukewarm cup of coffee to my lips and savoured a sip. It was so much better than the god-awful work blend we got. "This is nice, thank you."

"You're welcome." He drank from his mug. "But back to you... I'm..." The mug hit the coaster with a bang. "Sorry. I'm concerned for you. Really worried about what's going on inside you."

"Afraid I'll snap?"

"It's a legitimate concern but I can handle that. I can handle those emotions, as at least they are not being held inside." He twisted in his spot. "I just want to make sure you're okay. After everything that Murdoch did..."

I broke eye contact with him and allowed my gaze to roam around the living room, stopping to rest upon the top of the piano where a picture of an attractive lady with her arms around Liam sat. That must've been his wife. Seeing them together and knowing how her own demons drove a wedge between them when she wouldn't let him in, affected me. I didn't want to shut him out, but I didn't know how to let him in either. "How do I prove that I'm okay?" I flipped my focus to Liam for a heartbeat before I turned it back to the picture. "Because this isn't something you get over. Unfortunately, it stays with you and rears its head from time to time."

"My bad... wrong choice of words." He dropped his head into the palm of his hands. "I keep screwing up."

I tightened my grip around my legs and waited through a few breaths for him to explain.

"I just want..." He sighed and whispered under his breath, "Why is this so hard to say?" A sharp inhale. "I don't feel the need to protect you because I think you are weak or incapable." He gazed deep into my eyes. "I feel the need to protect you because you're important to me and I don't want you to be frightened. You need to know I would never hurt you."

My heart swelled ten times its size. How freaking sweet was he? I reached for his knee and gave it a tender squeeze. "I do know that. And I feel it more than your words say. Trust me on that."

"Whew. Okay." His shoulders rolled inward as he sat straighter. "I think it's important."

"What I can't understand is why though? Why me?"

"Because you make me smile."

I laughed out loud. It was the most ludicrous thing I've heard in a long while. "I make you smile?" I pointed at my chest. "Me?"

"You do. I love your enthusiasm with your students and the way you make each child matter."

"That's the job."

He shook his head. "It's more than that. You have an infectious nature. It's raw at the heart of it, but so amazingly beautiful when it blooms."

I cocked my eyebrow, totally not buying what he was trying to sell.

"I can see by that look that you don't believe me."

"You are 100% correct on that. I would say you've been deceived by some grand notion of some weird ideal. I'm not that person. At my core, I'm mean and heartless and incredibly selfish."

"Sure, you are." Those beautiful eyes of his did an impressive roll as he pressed into the sofa, handling his coffee as he went. "That's why you get along so well with everyone because you're mean and heartless." There was a smirk playing on the edges of his lip.

"It's an act."

"Yep. Sure."

"Truly it is."

"Then you must be one helluva a good actress to completely pull the wool over my eyes because I've been told I have a talent at reading people. And I've never been wrong."

Oh, this could be fun. "Really now?"

"Yep."

"Are you an empath too?"

"What do you mean?" He leaned forward and rested his elbows on his thighs.

"My friend is, although she denies it. She has this way of sensing what people are feeling."

"So, she's good at reading body language as well?"

I shook my head. "No, it's more than that. It's like she absorbs their feelings. If I'm sad, for instance, then she becomes ten times that and will cry for me. Or if I'm sick and throwing up, suddenly she's ill and ready to do the same."

"That's just creepy."

"That's the empath part of her. It's truly something to see it in action. Watch for it the next time you see her."

He chuckled. "I'm not an empath, that I can promise you. But I am good at reading people. Take Wentworth for example. Do you know him well?"

"I know enough." We weren't buddies or anything, but we had a good camaraderie at school.

"Okay. Wentworth." He rubbed his chin. "He's exceptionally closed-off personality-wise. He's a hard worker and is always pushing himself to be busy and to never take a break until his shift is over. I'm willing to bet, he's the same way at home. Do you know anything about his life away from work?"

I thought about it. He never mentioned anything, but then again, I'd never really asked. Former conversations rolled through my mind, tidbits here and there. Nope. Never once did he ever volunteer anything about his personal life. "That's just an educated guess. Besides, everyone knows he's a hard worker. That's not reading people, that's seeing it in action."

"Yet you mulled it over. I saw you thinking about it."

"Doesn't mean anything."

"My point is…" Those dark eyes of his penetrated right into my soul and I suddenly felt very naked and exposed. "I know what you're like and I've seen it, deep down. I like that part of you. That vulnerable and fragile part that you let slip without meaning to, the one that shows the true you." The sweetest smile I've ever seen on him spread across his kissable face and he leaned in closer.

"But she isn't real."

"Oh yes, she is."

My feet hit the thick rug that ran under the coffee table and I rose like I'd been zapped. I paced behind the couch and over to the piano, lifting the seat. There were dozens upon dozens of music sheets booklets.

"Would you like me to play something?"

I nodded but wasn't sure what. Most of the song titles meant nothing to me. "You pick."

"Fair enough." He rifled through the music sheets. "Do you know much about music?"

"What do you mean? Like the composers and stuff?"

He shook his head. "No, the emotional side of it. How music can change your mood? If you're in a sad mood, playing depressing music keeps you in that zone, but if you were to change the tone, your mood lifts." He slipped a sheet of music onto the holder in front of him.

"Sure." He really took things to a whole new level.

"And good music, powerful music, will give you goosebumps and you can't predict which music will do that, but when you find that one, cherish it. It doesn't have the same effect on everyone. And it's your soul that feels it."

I wanted to laugh. It sounded like bullshit, but I let him believe that I believed it. "Okay. Play me a piece that will give me goosebumps."

"I can't."

I knew he was lying.

"You need to find the one. I can play a dozen pieces, and none could sing into your heart, but I could also

242

play just one piece and it'll move you to tears."

"Try me." I had nothing to lose.

For an hour, Liam played various types of music; rock and roll, classical, jazz, the kind you'd play at a school concert. He finished the last notes and turned in my direction.

"You are a very talented piano player."

"Pianist," he corrected. He said it so fast it almost sounded like penis. Almost. "And those songs, what did you think?"

"I liked them. But no goosebumps. I thought it was close on the fifth or sixth song…"

He picked up the pile of papers and flipped through, setting them aside.

"But no. I didn't feel anything that was soul-piercing." It was a load of shit. I liked music as much as the next person, but never did it make my body react so viscerally.

"I just haven't found it yet. Or you truly are that cold and heartless." He laughed and turned towards the piano.

I tossed one of his throw pillows at him, hitting him in the back.

"Let's try this." He tapped a few keys. "I'm playing it from memory as the music sheets are with Dahlia as she's trying to jazz it up a bit and write the lyrics."

The music started playing, and a weird feeling started in my chest. It wasn't goosebumps but after he hit the melody, something resonated inside me. It was a slower song, but evenly paced. It had happier notes, interspersed with deeper sounds and a harmony that nearly rocked me to my core. Maybe I wasn't as heartless as I claimed. The last few notes touched me deep inside and reactionarily, I wiped my eyes as he finished up, but he caught me.

"Found it," he smirked. "Liked that song, do you?"

"My body does apparently." A lump formed in the back of my throat. "I suppose that means that the song has some special meaning behind it, and how if I looked at the words-"

"Lyrics."

"Lyrics," I corrected with a hint of snootiness, "if I looked at those *lyrics*, that they'd have some profound reasoning to them."

"Perhaps. Or it could be just the music. It doesn't have to be about the words, just how it makes you feel." He came to sit beside me. "And how did it make you feel? Are those tears of merriment or sadness?"

I swallowed the lump. "To me, it was like it started out all sad, but this lightness wove its way through, and it ended on a high note. Like a song about hope."

A shadow crossed over his face. "I wondered if you'd like it."

"So, what's the name of the song?"

"I don't know."

"How can you not know?"

"Because I'm still writing it."

Well, damn. "You wrote that?"

He nodded, and a swirl of pride and shyness settled over him. "Working on it. Dahlia and I are currently writing the lyrics. We'd planned on getting together this weekend since we have no shows booked."

"I can't wait to hear its full sound."

"Do you want to know the inspiration behind it?" He acted like a student who had done some artwork ready to show off to their parents.

"Sure."

"I wrote the melody for you." He walked over to the piano and played a few notes. "This was us in Mexico. All light and sunshine." The notes deepened and a sense of sadness filled the space. "And this is the past few days. I can see the fight in you and so much strength." Long fingers danced effortlessly over the keys. "The hope. Your spirit. See how it soars?"

The melody changed and it was hard to single out

245

an emotion to describe it. "You wrote a song based on us?" It was incredible to think this song had come from Liam's head, that he poured his personal thoughts deep into the musical notes.

"No, I wrote this song," his gaze fell to the keys, "for you."

Chapter Twenty-Five

I rose from the comfy spot on the couch and stepped over to the wonderful man with his chin tipped down. Bending over, I cupped his face in my hands and lowered my lips to hover over his. My body remembered the fantastic way he'd kissed me a lifetime ago in Mexico and it couldn't wait anymore. My eyes searched his out, watching for any signs of rejection or hesitation in his dark browns, and seeing none, I leaned in for the kiss.

Sweet baby Jesus it was everything I needed and fueled the dark with an intensity that drowned it out. Butterflies took flight in my gut and my core tingled with anticipation. What a remarkable sensation. I pulled back for air. "We're doing this." I reached for his hand and pulled him off the seat. "Where's your bedroom?"

In one fell swoop, he lifted me off my feet and walked to the door beyond the edge of the kitchen. We stepped inside and he put me down, my toes squishing into the softest, plushest carpet ever. It rivalled my thick bathroom towel.

"Are you sure?" Liam asked.

"I wouldn't have suggested it if I wasn't." I sauntered to the bed, my focus never leaving the sweet face before me.

Slowly, seductively, he pulled off his sweater and tossed it onto the back of the chair, leaving him in a plain white tee that highlighted the tan he got over spring break.

Not to be outdone, I removed the oversized sweater I'd changed into earlier, leaving me standing in leggings and a black lace bra. Glad I had the foresight to not swap that out for something more comfortable. This little number was magical, and it got Liam's gaze and held it for a few pounding heartbeats. Success.

He trailed a finger up my hand, over my arm, and across my collar bone, stopping just under my chin. "I want you to know that if you ever feel uncomfortable, you say the word and I'll stop immediately. Okay?" His gaze darted between my eyes.

"Okay." The words fell out breathlessly.

"Promise?"

"Liam, I'm okay." It was true. I felt it in every fiber of my being. Liam made me feel safe, there was no question about it. My hands ran the length of his muscular arms and down over the cottony material of his tee. On the hem, I pulled it up and over his head, admiring the physique of a man who was comfortable in his skin. It wasn't a hard six-pack I ran my fingers over, but it was taut and lean. And kissable. So kissable. I'd wanted to do this in Mexico, but he'd been the one to hold back and wait. Judging by the bulge in his pants, he was no longer going to wait. "Are you sure you want to do this?"

A hunger filled his eyes, and his expression softened. "Ever since the day I met you, Camille Evans."

"So why didn't you?" Does he know how hard it was to wait? To satisfy my own needs after we parted ways.

"Because you seemed…"

"Don't say different." Because I wasn't so different than the other girls at the resort.

"I wasn't going to. What I was going to say, if you could stop," he kissed my lips quickly, "interrupting me…" A lingering kiss on the side of my neck. "Is that you seemed…" Firm caresses swept across my lower back and his heated hand rested there and pulled me closer. "Real."

"Real?" And here I'd thought I'd been faking who I am all along.

"It was scary in its honesty. And I didn't want to

take advantage of that."

"Oh please," I begged in a voice heavy with desire. That need to feel more of his touch overwhelmed me. "Please, take advantage of me. I'm yours to have."

His lips silenced further words, and my chest fused to him while nimble fingers danced on my back and unhooked my bra. A moan slipped out, deep and guttural. There was a chance I'd come undone all on my own without his help if he kept caressing me like he was.

Like never before, fireworks shot out from my body with every touch, every lingering kiss, every stroke. The buildup to the sweet, intoxicating release was the most intense reaction I'd ever experienced. Slow and deliberate, his timing was enough to make my toes curl in heady anticipation but not enough to actually happen. Groans and grunts only fueled him on. My body tightened and sensing it, he'd slow his pace, kissing down my legs while resting my foot on the thickest part of his strong thighs.

Leaving me in a gloriously tortured holding pattern of sweet ecstasy, I returned the pleasure onto Liam, savouring every inch of the body I'd yearned to run my hands over. It was perfection in a less than a perfect-looking body, and yet, he was everything I wanted. His skin tasted like fresh fruit picked off a tree, and I licked him clean. Two could play his slow and meditative game.

But it didn't take long, and before I had a chance to truly claim him with my body, he lost control and surrendered to me.

Momentarily spent, he resumed his undivided attention on my body, the desire rebuilding at a pace I wasn't too familiar with. Words escaped me, and thoughts were as jumbled as a tornado crossing a barren field. Time stopped but also sped up. My body was on fire, until his breath blew across a spot he'd kissed, turning it cool to the touch. Waiting for the epic release that was sure to do me in was magnificent and killer, all in one. But the body can only handle so much and one gentle fingering touch with nary a stimulation sent me off like a bottle rocket launching into space. I shattered into a bazillion pieces.

After catching my breath, I wrapped him up and flipped him over onto his back. He was my pony and I needed a long, satisfying ride into town. Our bodies became one, like puzzle pieces finding the perfect match. His face held more desire and longing than I'd ever noticed, and I found myself captivated and linked to the man beneath me. The one who had the power to calm me, to see me in all my literal and figurative nakedness and yet still stay. Still respected me.

Holding his hands, he succumbed to my seductive power and shuddered under me, opening his eyes and taking me all in. It was a look I'd never noticed in a man, and it scared me straight. I leaned down and kissed his face, pulling us apart while I rolled in tight beside him.

He kissed the tip of my nose. "You were fantastic."

"I know." I laughed but it was true. There was no doubting my skills in the sack.

"I love that about you." A contented sigh blew out of him after he smiled. "I love you." The words were whispered, like an afterthought, and I wondered if they held any meaning. Was it something he always said after sex, or did he truly mean it?

He held me close and it didn't take long before the soft sounds of a welcomed nap filled his room.

How could he love me? He barely knew me. I certainly wasn't in love with him. Yes, he was sweet and romantic and everything I'd ever hoped for. He made me feel safe and secure, and I'd found myself surrendering to him while we had sex, something I probably couldn't have done with just anyone. But that wasn't love, was it? Love wasn't just a feeling, wasn't love everything?

The crystal-clear realization dawned on me. It was so blatantly obvious. He manipulated my emotions, and in doing so, caused me to fall in love with him. It had nothing at all do with Trey. Liam knew he wasn't the runner up, or the consolation prize. He was *the* prize.

I'd been so blind, and so wrapped in everything going on with Murdoch that I didn't see how he used my anger to better himself. The tears he gave to the officer, the repeated acts of kindness. It was all a ruse. How could he do that to me? Why do guys insist on playing head games with me? It wasn't enough for me to give them my body, they had to go and mess with my head? Liam at least got it backwards. He wormed his way into my heart and then bedded me.

I was such an idiot.

Liam was sound asleep, so I slowly wiggled out from under his arm, and grabbed my things strewn across the room. Walking naked through his house, I made my way over to the guest room, jumping into my leggings and putting my bra on. After I pulled my sweatshirt over my head, I grabbed my bag from the guest bedroom and snuck out the back door.

Chapter Twenty Six

The uber dropped me off at my apartment and I sulked up the stairs to my place. Thankfully, I didn't see Trey in passing, which I was worried would happen. His sixth sense was sharp, and he always tended to show at the wrong time.

Entering my apartment, I tossed the keys on the counter, eyes suddenly transfixed on the bottle of Jack Daniels. *I'm not an alcoholic. I'm not an alcoholic.* I didn't crave a drink like they did. The whiskey didn't call out my name. All it did was soothe my rattled nerves and that so wasn't the same thing. I didn't drink to get drunk; it just always happened that way.

"Fuck it."

I poured myself a glass and pounded it back. Walking over to the couch, I flopped down on it, missing the nice squishy feeling that was Liam's furniture. Mine now felt ancient and abused with its saggy springs and misshapen pillows. My place was a dump and would never be considered a home like his place was. The apartment was basic lodgings, pure and simple. Nothing here made it homey, no pictures on the wall, no fancy decorations, not even the scent coming off a candle. I'd have to save for months to refurnish and decorate and give it value, and I wasn't sure I was invested in changing that part of my life.

From the depths of my purse, I pulled out my phone and dialled Tess.

She answered breathlessly. "Camille? What's up?"

I squinted at the screen, trying to figure out her surroundings. Realisation dawned upon me. For the moment, I'd forgotten she was on a weekend getaway with Jon. "I'm so sorry. I'll call you later."

"Nuh-uh. Something's going on." She swiped her hair away from her pink-tinged cheeks.

"Seriously. It's not important."

"It is, or you wouldn't have called. I can sense the anguish in you."

"Okay, Yoda." I rolled my eyes. "Something happened at work today." I filled her in the minor details, enough to cover the bases.

The phone bounced as she readjusted herself. "Oh, Camille."

My blood curdled. That type of pity rocked me to my core. "There's more." I unloaded about Liam and his alcoholic accusation, and how he manipulated my feelings.

"Well, I'm not surprised by the first part."

"What? You're supposed to be my best friend." How dare she? I almost threw my phone across the room.

"We've had this discussion, remember? I've been suspecting for a while now that you have a slight drinking problem."

"If I may," a deeper voice chimed in and a shirtless Jon appeared on my phone.

Damn, they were in bed together and I interrupted.

"It sounds like this Liam guy is really into you."

"Not me, just my shortcomings. He's only interested in trying to fix the mistakes he made with his wife."

Tess gasped.

"Yep, that's right, he was married. Only," my voice fell, "she killed herself because of her Murdoch and Liam used that against me and somehow tricked me into falling for him."

Jon rubbed his whiskery chin. "Perhaps that's how you see it, but as a guy, from what you've stated, I think he's fallen for you. He doesn't want to change you; he wants to protect you."

"Yeah, he said something like that."

"Only guys who are deeply invested in their gals would do that." He beamed as he turned his head to Tess. "Someday I'll be there to hold your hand on a daily basis and whisper how important you are to me as you drift off to sleep."

I cleared my throat.

His focus returned to the phone. "Trust me, Camille, the dude loves you and he's in so far over his head that nothing else makes sense. Except you."

"But he used me."

Both Jon and Tess shook their heads.

"I think you're afraid of what you're feeling. This isn't about him; this is all on you. Why are you so afraid to be with him? You say you want him, and then when he admits the same, you high tail it out of there."

"It's not that simple, T-bird."

"Actually, it is. I think you're just afraid to let yourself be truly happy and see this through."

Jon pointed at himself. "Take me for example, I took a leap of faith with Tess, and not a day has passed where I'm not thankful for her. It was written in the stars."

I didn't want to say anything out loud in case I jinxed things, but I was sure Tess and Jon were going to find their Happily Ever After together, it was just a matter of time and logistics. "You were meant to find each other."

Tess chimed in. "And you don't think you and Liam were? You met a guy from Edmonton 3000 miles away and you had an instant connection on a different level than you've ever had with any other male. If that wasn't enough, he ends up working at your school. Of all the schools in the area, yours. Think about that for a moment."

"Coincidences happen all the time."

"Not like that." Tess shook her head before resting it on Jon's shoulder. They were seriously so cute together.

"I think what we should be asking her," Jon said, "is how she feels about him?"

"That's a complicated answer." I crossed my legs and stretched out on my crappy couch.

"Not when you really think about it. Either you do, or you don't." Jon had a smug look on his face and Tess smiled as one appeared on hers.

"So?" Tess asked.

"So what?" I'd be the first to admit that I was having feelings for the guy. Deep feelings, like love and all that. Things I'd never felt with Trey. Even just thinking about Liam's handsome face and the sweet way he looked at me caused the butterflies to swirl. The sparkle in his eyes. The way his hand held mine perfectly. How he respected my opinion on work matters and was sensitive to my needs, especially in the bedroom. A wave of heat warmed me recalling that. I shrugged. "Maybe."

"She does." Tess was nearly giddy with squeals. "I knew it."

"Big deal if I do."

"Seriously, if you feel the way I think you do, you'd be a shit to pass up what could be a wonderful experience."

"Thanks, Tess." I rolled my eyes. It wasn't the first time she called me a shit.

"I'm serious. He loves you; you love him. I don't see what's holding you back."

"Umm… how he manipulated me? How he's using me to fix his past mistakes with his wife?" I mean the list was a mile long.

"Help him get over her. Show him you're better than her. You're alive, she's long gone. I think he knows that but there's maybe a little fear in him that you're going to disappear. Either physically, like she did, or into the bottle you keep running to."

"Actually, she did disappear, didn't you?" Jon asked, staring through the camera and deep into my soul. "Did you at least leave a note?"

"Poor guy is probably losing his mind." Tess and Jon took off on a little conversation of their own.

"Hey, guys, I'm still here."

Tess pulled the phone close enough the flecks of colouring in her eyes were hard to miss. "Listen, Camille, cause I'm only going to say this once. I love you, but you'd better pull your head out of your ass and run back into his arms. We all bring baggage into a relationship, but the best of them deal with it and help the other. It's all about balance. And you're an idiot if you don't see that." If she were standing in my apartment, she'd have her hand on her hip, mother-like, wagging her finger at me. Who knew, maybe she was doing that. It was hard to tell over the phone. "Listen, you figure it out. I'm going to run and soak up as much time with my boyfriend as I can. I'll call you on Monday when I land."

I blew her a kiss and said goodbye to the pair of them before I hung up.

Now I needed to think through my future. What did I really want from my life? I didn't want the typical white picket fence and 2.3 kids. I wanted peace, security, and happiness. I wanted a man who loved me for being me, despite all the bad and weaker parts. I wanted a man who gave me butterflies and whose touch I missed the moment it wasn't there.

Liam was all those things, and I wanted him. I needed him. Badly. The hardest part was admitting that to him because I'd screwed up when I stormed away.

A couple of hours later, I found myself knocking on Trey's door.

"I figured it was you," he said, pulling it open, "you never buzz first."

It was a horrible attempt at humour. Of course, I never buzzed first. I didn't need to – I just descended the stairs in the building.

"Wow, what's bugging you? Normally my lame jokes make you smile." He ran his fingers through his clean hair and the pieces in front fell effortlessly over his forehead.

"I need someone to talk to."

"And Tess isn't available?" He cocked an eyebrow at me.

Normally, she was my first go to, but… "She's in Vegas, and I need a guy's opinion."

"Then I'm your guy. Come on in." He closed the door behind me.

"Am I interrupting anything?" Trey was dressed in clean clothes, ones that smelled like he just pulled them from the dryer. There was even a hint of body soap still clinging to him.

"No. Just watching the game." He grabbed the remote and muted the sound of the hockey game. "Like the new furniture?"

I was more than a little surprised to see his living room so neat and tidy. Gone was the old threadbare couch and the rusty patio chairs he used, and in its place was a nice couch and matching chair. Even the 1970s relic of a coffee table was upgraded to a ceramic tile and metal framed table with shelves. As I stared at the tv unit, it too was new.

"Someone's been shopping."

"Someone has discovered package deals. This was a clearance model set. All of it for the price of two car payments. Got delivered yesterday."

I looked around the living room. I had to admit, it was a big change. "I'm impressed."

"Thank you. Figured it was time to do some clean up in my life. Got to start somewhere. Oh, and since you're here..." He disappeared down the hall and returned a moment later with a bag. "These are your things."

I took the heavy bag from him, curious as to what was inside. Slowly, I opened it and pulled out a blanket.

"The first few times you stayed here, you wrapped yourself in it."

The memory on that was strong. It was made of

fleece and was so soft and cuddly. It provided me with just the right amount of heat. "But it's yours."

"It belongs to you. It always has."

"Thank you." I folded it and tucked it back into the bag.

"I'm sorry, you know. Sorry for not being a better boyfriend." He hung his head. "You deserve a dedicated guy."

"Why did you stray?"

He blew out a breath. "Honestly, I don't remember. It's like I have a fear of commitment or something." He sighed and leaned into the couch, stretching out and propping his feet on his new coffee table.

"We'll go with that." Personally, it was a cop-out and there was more to it, but it wasn't for me to voice anymore. We'd broken up and I was ready to move on. "The reason I'm here…" I inhaled and folded my hands on my lap. "This morning at school, I snapped. What with everything that happened, I lost it." I spent the next ten minutes with Trey's undivided attention and filled him in about everything that went down at school and at Liam's house.

"Where's your phone?"

It was an odd response, but I pulled it out of my pocket.

"Text him right now and let him know you are okay."

"What?"

"If you have any respect for him, and I do mean *any*, you will do that. Tell him you are okay. Tell him you're scared but need time to think. Don't just run away, Cammy. Don't make the same mistakes I did."

I scoffed. "You cheated on me; you never ran away."

"I made so many mistakes with you, and it cost me. Big time." Sadness filled his voice. "Do you respect Liam?"

"Of course, I do." We'd been through so much together.

"Then please, tell him you're okay." He rose from the couch and walked into his kitchen. "Even I've never left someone right after snogging."

Which was probably true, at least with me. But he was right. Tess and Jon were right. By running away, I was doing the very thing Liam had been afraid I'd do. Shut him out. And that wasn't what I wanted. I typed out a quick text to Liam.

Sorry for leaving abruptly. I needed to escape and think things through. Too many emotions overcame me and frightened me. I'm not drinking, if you're worried about that. I'm hanging out with a friend who's working things out with me. I'll call you later. I promise.

"Done." I turned my phone off. I wasn't expecting Liam to return my text.

"Good. If that were me, and you ditched right after snogging, I'd be friggin crushed."

"Really?"

"This may come as a surprise to you, but I do love you. In my own weird little way, I do."

My jaw would've hit the carpet had I not fought so hard to keep my mouth shut.

"I know, I never said it. Reason number fifty of why we're no longer together."

I tucked my legs underneath me and repositioned myself in the chair. This was the most honest Trey had ever been with me.

"Ever since you came home from Mexico, you've been different. And not because of the drinking, although that probably has something to do with it, but your deposition has changed." He tipped his head from side to side in a contemplative way. "Maybe it's that bad guy who attacked you, but I think it's more."

"I doubt it."

"Oh Cammy, if you could only see yourself the way others see you." He shook his head. "That night at the jazz club, you thought I was watching the lead singer but in truth, I was watching you. When I knew you weren't paying attention to me, you were smiling from ear to ear watching him. I knew that guy was your co-worker, and I knew he was the one you came home with."

What? All this time...

"It's been a long while, and maybe it never happened, but I'm pretty sure you've never looked at me the way you looked at him. And even more... I know I've never seen you so happy, even if was only for a moment. Your drinking took that shine away though."

I hadn't realised that Liam had subconsciously lit me up. That night at the bar, I tried very hard to be serious, but listening to Liam play the piano, it moved me. Even today when he played. It was like seeing right into his soul. "You're not the first person to bring that up."

"And I won't be the last. Your drinking is getting out of hand, isn't it?" He scooted closer to me. "Be honest."

All the bottles of hard liquor. The full glasses I'd pounded back. Falling asleep in the tub, that night should've been a wakeup call, I could've died, and Liam would really have a hard time. I went to open my mouth, but Trey covered it with his finger.

"I see the anguish in your eyes. Don't bare your

soul to me, bare it to Liam. He deserves it more than I do. If you let him into that part of yourself, you can fix this. You deserve that kind of happiness, even if you think you don't."

Tears filled my eyes. "Thank you, Trey."

"Also, make him something special. Something he can't say no to."

"Any ideas?" I wiped under my eyes.

Trey laughed. "I brought home four trays of lasagna if you'd like one."

I wasn't sure that would do it, but I took one home for myself anyways. Trey was a great cook and had proven that he was a good friend too.

Chapter Twenty Seven

J swallowed down the nervousness sitting at the back of my throat. As confident as I was about what I had planned, my nerves were shot. Sorting out my life wasn't nearly as much fun as I hoped, especially since I'd stayed mostly dry. Only twice did the taste of alcohol touch my lips, and each time, I set aside. A clear head was a must, even if it meant facing some ugly thoughts. I'd even conjured a list of positive reasons for what I was about to do, which surprisingly, completely outweighed the only negative thought – that he'd slam the door in my face and that would be the end of it.

I'd hoped it wouldn't come to that, but I was prepared for it, just in case. Over the past two days, I realised how much I'd fallen for Liam. He was in every thought, every movement and as much as I wanted a drink, I wanted him more.

I parked at the end of his street; eyes glued on his place which was two houses away. It was Easter Sunday, a day for new beginnings and I intended on making a new beginning.

I locked my car and strolled down the block in a beautiful flowy dress I'd purchased yesterday. It screamed summer, and I was rushing the season a little as it wasn't warm enough to be outside sleeveless. But it was gorgeous and would go well with dinner, if I was still invited as the random guest of the year. Inhaling a breath of courage, I reminded myself I was in control—for now—as I was about to surrender it completely in a few moments.

Breathing quickly, I rang the doorbell and heard the footsteps as he approached and opened the main door.

A lighthearted feeling settled over me at seeing his rugged face, but in a heartbeat, it was wiped away. Liam bore a scowl as his gaze washed over me.

"Wait," I said before he could close the door. "Please, let me explain." A breeze ruffled my slightly curled hair, blowing it off to the side. "Can I come in?" He still hadn't opened the screen door.

"Just for a minute, I need to leave right away."

"For Easter dinner, right?"

He nodded.

I didn't want to be quick, but his closed-off stance

had me questioning if what I was doing was right. Maybe my timing was off. "I was miserable all weekend and I missed you so much."

He shoved his hands into the depths of his pockets but didn't say a word.

Great. I was going to be the only one talking. That's fine, it had been part of my preparation. I was the one who screwed up royally, and it was all on me to fix it. "For starters... Would it be okay if I sat down?" He nodded slowly and I walked over to the couch. As if he could read my mind, he sat beside me. "I've spent a lot of time thinking. Over and over I went over our conversations and replayed them. On Friday, I'd somehow convinced myself that I was only a replacement for your wife. That you were trying to fix whatever mistakes you made."

He pursed his lips together, and instantly guilt swarmed me.

"That's not the right words. You didn't make a mistake with her." I shook my head. "What was her name?" How horrible was I that I'd never asked before?

"Teresa."

I turned to look at her picture. Yep, she looked like a Teresa, a beautiful name for a beautiful woman. However, she was gone. "Sadly, the fault lies with Teresa. For whatever reason, her demons controlled her. They lied to her, convinced her she was better off not being around."

He scowled. "How would you know that?"

I inhaled and let my gaze fall to my lap, trying to wipe my sweaty palms on my skirt without it looking like that's what I was doing. "I know that because…" This was so hard. I bit my lip and sighed. "Because that's what my demons were doing to me." I hesitated to look at him, not wanting to see a look of pity on his face. When I finally sucked up the courage to peek, there wasn't pity or disgust, there was genuine concern and sympathy. Seeing that unravelled me a little. "They'd convinced me that you were only interested in me because you needed a new project to do, someone new to fix. It twisted your words."

"Did it ever."

"And then there was the accusation of my drinking problem." Unable to watch his expression change, I shifted my gaze to the wall behind him, staring at the painting of horses in a pasture. "I don't know if I am an alcoholic or not, but I don't feel that I fit the typical definition. I don't consume it at work, and it's never affected my job performance. I don't drink and drive and would never." I swiped my hand through the air. "Never mind, I'm making excuses and not seeing the big picture. However, since I left here on Friday evening, I've only had two tastes of alcohol. That's it. I didn't want a cloudy head to impair my thoughts, everything needed to be crystal clear. And that's when it hit me. I realised how I don't have a drinking problem per se so much as I have a Liam problem."

He snorted but didn't move. Good sign.

"And it's a problem that only you can help fix. You're someone that I can't be without. All weekend long, the booze was there ready to fill in the wounds and wipe away all the hurt and heartache and bad memories. But you weren't, and I wanted you more."

The lines on his forehead deepened as he took in my words.

"All my life, I've been let down by more people than I care to admit, and truth be told, I know I've let them down too. But not everyone, not Tess. My parents for sure, boys in general, even some girls in school and at work. Even Trey had let me down repeatedly and yet, for some strange reason, I hung on to him with all that I had, figuring that was better than nothing. But it's not. That was my demons at play, convincing me that sub-par was the best I was ever going to get. Until I met you. It's like Fate was trying to show me better was out there."

All his attention was on me, and normally, I'd be trying to get away from it, but this is what I wanted.

"From that moment you amused me by pretending to be the poolside server and brought me the drinks I'd ordered, I haven't been able to get you out of my head, and more recently I haven't been able to get you out of my heart. You entered my life at the wrong time, and yet, everything about it was timed perfection. You saw the worst of me, the broken parts that I haven't even let my best friend see. You didn't run like you should've. You stayed. You put up with me. You gave me something I never knew I needed."

"Oh yeah?"

"Yeah. You give me hope. Such a weird and intangible thing, and yet it's always with you and it seeped into me. Being around you doesn't just make me a better person; it makes me real. You make me feel things I never thought was possible, feelings I'd resigned to thinking belonged to people like Tess and Jon. And yet, with you, there's hope for a better tomorrow, for more of what you do to me."

"Like piss you off?" It was said in a teasing tone, but still.

"I'm trying to be romantic here and you're killing my vibe."

A smile widened, stretching from ear to ear, and he waved me on. "I'm sorry. Carry on. But spoiler alert, I'm liking what I'm hearing so far."

"I'm going to get help, professional help." It was

in my calendar to discuss with Saunders about the mental health sessions I knew I needed. "I'm totally okay with you choosing to not be with me as I go through it. It's going to get ugly and nasty and ghosts I've tried locking away will finally be set free. I don't know how long it will take, but I promise you, I'll be waiting for you on the other side, if you'll still want me."

He shook his head and my heart stopped beating. "I'm not going to want to wait for you."

Can't say I didn't try.

"I want to be there with you while you go through it. I want to be your strength when you feel weak. I want to be your hope when you feel it's all gone."

"Oh, Liam." Tears burst out of me. "Are you sure?"

"With all my heart."

"Oh good, that makes what I'm going to say next so much easier." I wiped my eyes, thankful for having the foresight to apply waterproof mascara. Dropping onto one knee, I pulled out the ring I'd chosen for him.

His expression fell and his eyes widened.

"William Donaldson, your honesty and the way you don't hide your emotions from me is refreshing. Your love for me is pure and fascinating. You want to protect me and care for me, and in the deepest parts of me, I need to do the same for you. You are the other half I swore I'd never find, and the timing into my life couldn't have been worse. But you're here. You stayed. I love you, Liam and I want you in my life for as long as you'll have me." I lifted the golden band to him. "Don't get too wrapped up in this, it's only a promise ring."

A loud whoosh breathed out of him. "Thank god. It's way too soon for that."

I laughed while nodding. "Agreed. I'm just asking if you'll let me commit myself to you. For as long as you'll have me."

His brows knit together, and his eyes searched out the truth in my soul. If he looked hard enough, he'd see the truth laying there naked in all its glory. The warmth of his hands wrapped around mine, silencing their trembling. A quick nod. "Yes."

"Yes?"

"Yes, I want you in my life for as long as you'll have me too." His hands stroked my arms and cupped my face. The sweetest kiss, filled with the biggest heart, touched my lips like a feather against the skin.

I pressed into him and wrapped my hands around him, holding him in as close as humanly possible.

He pulled away first. "I know I'm not perfect, and I have my own issues of not being able to let go of Teresa, but I'm trying."

"I'm okay with that. She was a part of your life; I'd never expect you to wipe her from it."

He squeezed my hand. "I know I can't always protect you, but damn it, I'm going to try. Just a heads up though, I'll ask too many questions and I'll be super clingy, but it's only because I love you and want the best for you."

"I want the best for you as well. I promise to be honest with you about what I'm feeling and to watch how I'm drinking and if it's because I'm trying to numb my emotions, I'll let you know."

"That's all I ask."

"I love you, Liam."

"I love you, Camille." He pulled me onto my feet, and popped the ring out of the box, handing it to me.

With love, I slipped it onto his right hand, it was a promise ring after all, and not an engagement ring.

"Boy, won't my parents be surprised." He laughed. "And your friend Tess."

"Ah, she already knows."

He winked. "Of course, she does."

"She knew it was coming." I swept my long dress off the floor. "Now, take me to your parent's house. I can't wait to meet the people who gave you life and raised the wonderful man I've fallen in love with."

"Oh, Camille." He swept me off my feet and planted the most passionate kiss on my lips. "I can't wait to show you off, they're going to love you almost as much as I do."

Epilogue

$\mathcal{M}$y feet dragged through the plush carpeting of the bedroom. Today was the day. It was finally happening, and I couldn't be more nervous.

Liam exited the bathroom, dressed in a fine suit. "You look gorgeous."

"I feel like I'm going to rattle myself apart." I lifted my trembling hands to show them off. Leaves in a windstorm shook less.

"I promise, it'll be okay. If the sentencing hearing goes well, he'll be behind bars for a helluva long time."

I nodded, knowing that was the outcome we'd all be hoping for.

Filing for my restraining order had opened Pandora's box. Two other staff members came forward and shared their stories. They hadn't reached my level of intimate contact, but one had been kissed. After the incidents at the school, the disappearance of Edalyn came to light, via a gossip-loving parent who worked at the hospital. Unfortunately, Murdoch took out his rejection on her, and she was in the hospital the day of the office incident. He'd done to her what I imagined he would've done to me that Monday afternoon had we not been interrupted.

My heart broke for her. Multiple times over.

Murdoch was arrested and detained. Edalyn pressed charges, and upon hearing that, I joined her. Seventeen months after that horrible day, today was the day the bastard would be going to jail. And I wasn't missing that, as shaky as I was.

"Court's at ten, we'd better get going." I grabbed my purse and walked through the kitchen, stopping at the sight. A beautiful bouquet of flowers sat in the middle of our table, brightening the space with the gorgeous hues of rose red, sunflower yellow and leafy greens. The card on it read: *Go get him. Love Trey and Melissa.*

In a move that surprised everyone, Trey had stopped cheating and hooking up with every female that showed the slightest interest. He'd cleaned up his life and had found his true connection in Melissa, a beautiful, spunky redhead. They'd been dating over the past six months. He'd recently shared with me that he thought she was the one. Seeing him so happy, moved me to tears. Trey deserved that level of happiness.

"Come on, we're going to be late." Liam tugged me away from the flowers.

The ride to the courthouse, I read and re-read my victim impact statement, four pieces of paper filled with emotion about the effects of his wrongdoing and the after affects on my life. It was worse than the AA introduction meeting, which I stopped attending after that. I haven't stopped drinking in its entirety, but I've really slowed down, and for me and Liam, that was a huge start.

The statement curled and uncurled in my hands, the sweat softening it more than the crumpling.

"I'll be able to stand with you, remember?"

"I know." Edalyn's lawyers had gone over that a few times to prep me. I'd only attended one session of court, the day Edalyn took the stand. Of all the court times to attend, I'd picked the day where the most graphic details would emerge. It turned my stomach, but I was happy to show Edalyn I was there to support her.

It was a long walk to the law court building from the parkade, and time felt like it was standing still. Eventually, we made it and stopped just outside the doors to Courtroom 417.

Liam's fingers laced through mine. "Breathe.

You've got this." He lifted my hand now sporting its own engagement ring and planted a kiss on my knuckles.

I inhaled a long breath and closed my eyes, slowly nodding and convincing myself this was almost over. "Okay, I'm good."

Liam opened the door and I led the way inside. On my way to the front row of the gallery, I spotted Dale and Mandi Donaldson—Liam's parents, Janet and her husband Rick, Tess and Jon, Izabella and her newlywed husband, and of course a few staff members, notably Wentworth.

"You're never alone," Liam whispered as we walked over.

Gratefulness bubbled out from inside me, and I nearly spilled over my words. "Thank you everyone for being here. You have no idea what this means."

Tess winked. "Oh, I think I do."

Hands squeezed my shoulders and hugs from my surrogate family wrapped around me. I'd never felt so strong and ready to take on the world.

I leaned into Liam and whispered, "Once this is done, I think we should move to discuss our future."

Tess leaned forward and patted my shoulder. "Put my vote down for a double wedding in Mexico."

"Vegas is better," Izabella said in a light laugh and squeezed her husband's hand.

Entertaining both suggestions, I nodded. If I was going to get married, it either needed to be immediate or wait eight months. I didn't want a baby bump in my wedding photos. Just an hour ago I took a pregnancy test. The two lines were as clear as the picture on the box.

Now I just needed to find a grand way to surprise him with the news.

Before I could fully open that proverbial door however, I needed to close another.

One by one, the lawyers filed in. A meek and fearful looking Edalyn walked beside her lawyer, her family reaching out to touch her hand and whisper words of encouragement. Next Murdoch was escorted in, lawyers on either side of him and a security guard within a foot's grasp.

The bailiff barked out, "All rise," and immediately our group silenced themselves.

The judge, a surly man who looked like he might already have one foot in the grave, walked in. "Please be seated and let's begin."

IT ALL
BEGAN
with a wedding

Thursday – June 11th

I was minutes away from becoming the major shareholder of a national chain of pharmacies. I was minutes away from becoming richer than I ever dreamed. I was minutes away from my life changing forever. The worst part was, I wanted nothing to do with it.

"Miss Richardson, are you hearing what I'm saying?" The oldest-looking of the three men pulled off his wire-rimmed glasses, and with his other hand rubbed the bridge of his nose.

"Yes, sir."

"Would you care to repeat it back to me? This is a very important matter and it's imperative that you fully understand." He glanced to the other two people; each one sitting on the other side of him – all three staring across the table at me.

Carefully, and with the intent of coming across as much older than my twenty-seven years, I nodded. "If I'm to understand you correctly…" I glanced at the folders lined up neatly between us. "I am about to inherit my grandfather's shares of his pharmaceutical company Merryweather-Weston."

I didn't add that it was a company my grandfather Lloyd Merryweather started from the ground up in his late teens in the 1960's. When he married my grandmother Thelma Weston in 1965, he added her name to the business. Together, over the past fifty years, they grew their mom and pop corner store into a nationwide chain.

"That's correct." He reached for a file and opened it to a pinned page. "Go on."

I kept my sighs to myself. "As the, how did you put it, shareholder with the largest interest, I will hold 58% of the company's shares and stocks which are currently held in the family trust."

My math was rusty and the numbers I'd written down at the start of the meeting were swimming around on the page. All I knew was that by having more than fifty percent, I was in charge, another thing I wasn't looking forward to. Running a business was so beyond my learning capabilities. Why hadn't Grandpa bothered to discuss this with me previously?

Oh right. He wasn't supposed to have been killed.

An older gentleman, originally introduced as the accountant, who sat next to the lawyer, scribbled across a legal pad. "The correct percentage is 58.3." He didn't lift his eyes to make contact with me.

That's what that number was. I circled it repeatedly to drive that home. Percentages with decimals were a big deal. As I looked around the boardroom, I was so out of my league, and every person in that room knew it. Growing up the way I did, I wasn't expected to follow in my single mother's footsteps and eventually run the business the way she had, not even when cancer took her away four years ago. She'd been on board though when I felt a calling into micro-biology and creating new drugs that would cure various illnesses. I wanted to be famous for finding a cure for cancer, not running a well-known business.

Instead of toiling away in the lab, I was sitting with a lawyer, an accountant and whoever the third guy was, forced to take ownership of the entire three thousand plus stores. Although the way they talked about the whole situation, it was already a done deal. They just needed my signature on a bunch of papers to make it official.

"Just so you're aware, Mr. Crowe, I know–"

"We are aware of your position, Miss Richardson.

With Mr. Merryweather's accident, this has been thrust upon you. The board of directors are willing to assist you however they can until you get on your feet, and the CFO is on board to bring you up to speed. This meeting is just to sign over the documents that will make you the new President and owner."

I cleared my throat. "And if I decide that I don't want to be the president of the company?"

I belonged in the lab, wearing latex gloves and eye goggles, not in a boardroom, running a company. However, with my family all gone, it appeared like I had little choice in the matter.

That blank expression the lawyer had for the last hour hadn't faded with my admission. "You are free and clear to sell off your shares as you see fit, after first offering them to the shareholders and then to the board of directors." He flipped through a stack of papers and retrieved a stapled package and set it in front of me.

There was so much I needed to learn. Why did Grandpa have to drive that day? If he'd only taken a ride from his service... I shook my head, feeling a tendril of hair sneak out of the clip and fall across the nape of my neck. So much for maintaining a professional look.

"Miss Richardson," said the only man in the room who really hadn't talked much over the past hour. So many different terms had come and gone that I couldn't remember what his position was. "If I may." He pulled himself closer to the table and set down his pen. "This is a difficult time for you, and we're all aware how much information you are being bombarded with."

At least someone had the decency to understand.

"In simple terms, you are now the sole owner of your grandfather's company and you can be as involved as you wish. However, any changes you'd like to implement must pass through the shareholder's board. The twelve members collectively hold the other 41.7% of the business. None of that will change, unless you wish to sell part or all of your shares. The only thing that has changed, at this point in time, is the name on the title. Merryweather-Weston will continue to operate in its excellent way with or without your input."

My head was swirling with words and numbers and visions of a stuffy board room similar to the one I was in and a future where I'd be swimming with the sharks. Oh, how I needed to escape, even if just for a moment to catch my breath. There were no windows up here, no view to take in. Just dark grey walls giving the whole room an institutional feel. I twitched in my seat and buried my head in my hands. "I'm sorry, I just need time to process all of this. To be honest, I thought I was coming here to sign a few papers." I wanted to add and *go my merry* way but refrained and bit my lip instead.

The lawyer broke his staidness and cocked an eyebrow in my general direction.

The last guy pulled back another file with a tab that had my name on it and opened it. A stack of papers at least a half inch thick were neatly tucked inside. Were those all on me?

An unknown and unwelcome tightness squeezed around my chest.

A knock sounded on the door.

"Come in," the lawyer said.

A middle-aged man in a form-fitting suit walked in and dropped another file on the table. "Sorry to interrupt, but we found some information that changes the presidency of the company."

"Miss Richardson, this is Mr. Colby Pratt, one of the board members."

Mr. Pratt shook my hand with a giant Cheshire cat grin and turned his attention back to the lawyer. I'd never met the man previously, but his name was one tainted from overhearing Grandpa discuss business over the phone when he was at home. Mr. Pratt name did not come with the affection of a grandfather talking with a grandson, instead it was met with disdain. Grandpa wanted Mr. Pratt out of the business but he refused to sell.

"What did you find out?"

Mr. Pratt did not glance in my direction. "At the time of Ms. Nora Weston's passing, Mr. Merryweather updated his last will and testament and named Miss Richardson here as the sole inheritor."

Nora Weston was my mother, their former CEO who was as tough as nails.

"We have already established that."

"However, those shares are to be halved." Mr. Pratt puffed out his chest, straining the buttons on his already too-tight shirt. "As a lawyer, how did you not check out Miss Richardson's person?" He narrowed his eyes. "According to the Matrimonial Property Act, her shares would be equally split between her and husband, effectively diluting the ownership. With that division, including her shares owned previously, she would own 34.45% of the shares. As a shareholder with a personal share total of 35%, that would mean I'd become president." He pushed a stapled copy of papers in the lawyer's direction.

Matrimonial Act? Was that something that worked out between Grandpa and Grandma? No wait a minute, he was referring to *my* shares. But I wasn't married.

I still hadn't even found the guy I'd want to share

anything personal with, let alone spend the rest of my life with. Married? The idea was crazy enough to make me laugh. But I held back.

Wait a minute!

Images flitted through my mind at light-speed. A cute guy. A convention back in the fall. Way too much booze.

The lawyer lifted the new document and flipped through them. "But she hasn't announced an engagement, Mr. Pratt. I think you're jumping the gun just a little, and if she were to get married, she can, and should, get a prenuptial." He looked down his nose at me.

"She's already married."

Everyone knew that marriages in Vegas were a farce. There needed to be a license and all that. One can't simply go into any old chapel and get married without those things. Otherwise, it's like performing a part of a play; it wasn't real.

Mr. Michael's stupid grin got even bigger when he turned to me.

I balled my hands into tight little fists. Fight with the truth, Grandpa said, and you'll always win. "It wasn't legal." I inhaled, trying to calm myself. "Where's the marriage license?"

Mr. Pratt flipped through his file and dropped a

single piece of paper on the table between the lawyer and myself.

Clear as a bell on a beige wedding certificate from the Cupid's Arrow Chapel was my name and the name of one Theodore Breslin.

That drunken night at a Vegas medical conference flashed through my mind again. There was no way anyone would've married us, we were too drunk to know how to spell our names, as evident in the spelling of mine. On the certificate, my name was spelled I-S-A-B-E-L-L-A, but in truth, the 's' was a 'z'.

The buttons on my blouse pulled against their holds as I inhaled rapidly. I couldn't be married. It can't be possible. I haven't even seen that guy since then.

"Miss Richardson?" The lawyer's voice seemed far away as if caught in a fog.

My hand wiped the building sweat off my forehead, taking all my composure with it. "Yeah?" Grandpa would've smacked my backside for answering an elder like that.

"I guess that solves your dilemma."

"What's that?"

"You said you didn't want to be president, and now you don't have to worry about that. You'll remain on board as a minor shareholder, but not the president."

It sounded as if I should've been happy about the news of a marriage to a guy I didn't recall saying I do to, but the smug look on Mr. Pratt's face wiped away the smidgen of joy I may have held for the briefest of heartbeats. Not only did he resemble a weasel, he acted like it too. A burst of adrenaline coursed through me. Yeah, maybe I didn't want to run the company, but I'll be damned if I was going to turn it over to him. Grandpa really disliked him.

I faced the lawyer. "If I get a divorce, how does that work?"

"By law, if there was no prenup, he'd still be entitled to half."

Right, that whole Matrimonial Act and all. That wouldn't solve issue number one. I needed to think. A drunken marriage. I was sure there were more of those than not. How many ended up not being legit? Probably low. I tapped my head. Wasn't there a celebrity who married in Vegas and got it annulled? "What about an annulment? Then that would dissolve the marriage and all assets remained would be mine, correct?"

Mr. Pratt's face fell. Good.

The lawyer shuffled a few papers around and scribbled on his legal pad. "Provided you and..." He reached for the marriage certificate. "Mr. Breslin met certain criteria."

"Like? Is being drunk enough to not remember reason enough?"

"It stacks the deck in your odds." He finally made eye contact with me but after first glancing up at Mr. Pratt.

The prick had the audacity to laugh. "She'll never get in front of a judge in time."

"Why's that?"

"Because Miss Richardson…" He opened his file and flipped to a page tagged with a yellow tab. "If you'd read section 198.14, and I'll summarize this for you, it basically states that even though the estate is frozen, there is a 60 day grace period to find an interim president. With your assets now in half, I legally become the president, and there are only fifteen days left to contest." I could almost imagine Grandpa saying he'd smack that look off the smug bastard's face. The thought made me smile.

"Well, let's get that process started, so I can get before a judge. I'll need a minute with you, in private, please," I addressed the lawyer.

"Absolutely."

An hour later, I left the high rise building in the heart of our downtown a different person. Not only was I married, but I had a less than two weeks to find my husband, get an annulment before the judge Mr. Filewick had graciously set up for me, and retain major shares in the business I barely understood in order to keep Mr. Pratt's greasy little hands off it. Over a couple of hours, I'd aged ten years.

Dear Reader

So, how was Camille and Trey and Will? Did the right couple end up together? To me, they sure did. What did you think of Camille? A little bit of a fighter? She was a bit tougher to write than Tess in book 1, or Izabella in book 3. Camille has a dark past, and although I only scraped the surface, you can probably see what she's concealing. I hope you liked her, maybe not as much as Will, but still. LOL. Does your mental image of her match the cover? As soon as I hired my cover designer, she sent me hunting and I found the couple on the cover and my mind was blown! To me, they were Camille and Will, and I couldn't have found a more perfect looking couple.

Up next is Izabella's lighter-hearted story, due for release on Sept 15th. Follow my facebook and twitter pages for all the fun!

As an author, it makes my day when a reader shares their thoughts on the novel they've invested their time in. When readers fall in love with a character, it's encouraging to write more. Fun fact, when I finished writing *Duly Noted* and released it, a lot of readers wanted to know more about the friendship between Lucas and Aurora, and because of those emails, *That Summer* came to be.

So, if you don't mind, share with me what you liked, what you loved, or even what you hated. I'd love to hear from you, and I appreciate all my reviews & ratings on your favourite retailer site. They help gain visibility, and as I'm sure you can tell from my books, reviews are tough to come by. If you have the time for an extra review, please post one on Goodreads.

Thank you so much for spending time with me.

Yours,

H.M. Shander

Other Books

By USA TODAY bestselling author H.M. Shander

Duly Noted – book 1
That Summer – book 2
If You Say Yes – book 3
Serving Up Innocence
Serving Up Devotion
Serving Up Secrecy
Serving Up Hope
It All Began with a Note
It All Began with a Mai-Tai
It All Began with a Wedding
Noel
Whistler's Night
Dreamers in Cheshire Bay
Return to Cheshire Bay
Adrift in Cheshire Bay
Awake in Cheshire Bay
Christmas in Cheshire Bay
Journey to Cheshire Bay
Charmed in Cheshire Bay
Second Chances in Cheshire Bay
Unforgiven in Cheshire Bay
Flirty in Cheshire Bay
Up to Date listings can be found on the website.
www.hmshander.comt

Acknowledgements

This is my twelfth thank you in the back of a book, and I swear, writing the thanks yous never gets easier. Always afraid I'll miss someone, or a category will be left out. And then I wonder, does anyone even read these? I know as an author, I do, but I wonder if readers do? Do you? Writing a book, is a solo endeavor (for me at least), but I could not have this ready for you to read if not for the cheerleading and support of some magnificent people in my life.

First – my Shander family, whom you may know on my social media platforms as Hubs, The Teen, and Little Dude. Thank you from the bottom of my heart for letting me pursue what I love doing, for something that allows me to transport myself to another time and place. Thank you for cheerleading as I had a sale and watching the numbers climb, and the ranking scale up. Thank you for encouraging me to keep going and to chase my dreams, and for the nonstop coffees I sometimes needed when I was on a role. I love you all with my whole heart. With this novel I set out for a prestigious goal, and I'm over the moon to have achieved it. Thank you for being with me as my dream finally came true.

To my parents and in-laws and extended family – Thank you for your support, endless cheerleading, and encouraging your friends and family to give my books a try. Having you visit me at markets and book signings means the world. I have an amazing family, and every day I'm thankful to you all. Thanks for being you.

To my wonderfully dedicated alpha reader – Mandy. As soon as those first chapters are written, you are my go-to person. You let me know what worked, what wasn't, and if those opening lines, pages and chapters were enough to hook a reader into wanting more and I'm so appreciative of that. It's great having you to bounce an idea or two (or a couple hundred) and you are such a fantastic mentor and cheer squad. I heart you more than you'll ever know.

To my fantastic beta reader & critique partner – Josephine. Thank you for spending your free time reading my words and pointing out what didn't make sense and what needed to be expanded on, and how you enjoyed Camille's feistiness. Your critiques were as welcome as your enthusiasm. It's great having you in my corner and I hope you'll want to read the next MS I have sitting in the wings.

To my cover designer –When that first cover image came in, my mind was blown. You captured the essence of the story. I'm so thrilled we worked on this together, and I look forward to many more covers designed by you.

To my editor – Irina. Thanks for your dedication to fixing my errors and highlighting the inconsistencies.

To the other authors in the Romantically Ever Set – it was a great run! I learned so much from all of you and I've made some new friends. I can't believe we made list, especially when the whole Zon fiasco happened. Goes to show you what a bunch of angry women can accomplish.

If I missed you, it certainly wasn't intentional. I know I couldn't be where I am without the help of so many others. Thank you! And thank you for reading and making it all the way to the end. You all rock.

About the Author

H.M. Shander is a star-gazing, romantic at heart who once attended Space Camp and wanted to pilot the space shuttle, not just any STS – specifically Columbia. However, the only shuttle she operates in her real world is the #momtaxi; a powerful electric car that transports her two kids to school, work, and various sporting events. When she's not commandeering Elektra, you can find the elementary school librarian surrounded by classes of children as she reads the best storybooks in multiple voices. After she's tucked her endearing kids into bed and kissed her trophy husband goodnight, she moonlights as a contemporary romance novelist; the writer of sassy heroines and sweet, swoon-worthy heroes who find love in the darkest of places.

If you want to know when her next heart-filled journey is coming out, you can follow her on Twitter(@HM_Shander), Facebook (hmshander), or check out her website at www.hmshander.com.
Thanks for reading– all the way to the very end.

www.ingramcontent.com/pod-product-compliance
Lightning Source LLC
Chambersburg PA
CBHW020229260626
47156CB00002B/606